Somersaults
— and —
Dreams

Somersaults
— and —
Dreams

MAKING
★ THE ★
GRADE

CATE SHEARWATER

DEAN

DEAN

Somersaults and Dreams: Making the Grade
First published in Great Britain 2015 by Farshore
This edition published 2021 by Dean
An imprint of HarperCollins*Publishers*
1 London Bridge Street, London SE1 9GF
www.farshore.co.uk

HarperCollins*Publishers*
1st Floor, Watermarque Building, Ringsend Road
Dublin 4, Ireland

Text copyright © 2015 Cate Shearwater
Illustration copyright © 2015 Jongmee
The moral rights of the author and illustrator have been asserted.

ISBN 978 0 0085 1738 0
Printed and Bound in the UK using 100% Renewable Electricity
at CPI Group (UK) Ltd
001

A CIP catalogue record for this title is available from the British Library.

Typeset in Sabon by Avon DataSet Ltd, Bidford on Avon, Warwickshire

Stay safe online. Farshore is not responsible for content hosted
by third parties.

MIX
Paper from
responsible sources
FSC™ C007454

This book is produced from independently certified FSC™ paper
to ensure responsible forest management.

For more information visit: www.harpercollins.co.uk/green

For Elsie and Lucy
and all the wonderful gymnasts and
coaches at Baskerville's Gym Club.
With all my love.

CHAPTER
One

Ellie stood on the beach and stared out across the creek. The pale winter sun was just rising over the water and everything was still, except the gentle bob of the boats and a solitary seagull looping in the air. It reminded her of a gymnast turning circles on the bar.

She shivered with excitement and cold. The day she'd been dreaming of for so long was finally here! She'd woken up early, far too excited to sleep. So she'd slipped out of bed, taking care not to wake her little sister Lucy, pulled on her flip-flops and stolen down to the beach in her pyjamas

and duffle coat. She didn't want to waste a second of this day.

The water sparkled under the sun and Ellie gave a little sigh. She knew she was going to miss this place like mad. But she was going to the Academy! She had won a place at the London Gymnastics Academy, the best gym in the whole country, where famous gymnasts like Sian Edwards and Emma Bannerdown and even the great Lizzie Trengilly, Ellie's aunt, had trained.

Just thinking about it made Ellie want to somersault with joy. She grinned as she looked around. There was no better place for somersaults than the beach.

So Ellie kicked off her flip-flops, shrugged out of her duffle coat and prepared to launch herself into a tumble sequence across the cold, damp sand. She started with a simple round-off flick, then sprang into a neat aerial – like a cartwheel with no hands. The chill wind caught in her hair as she moved, and she could almost imagine she was leaping across the ice-cold water.

'I should have guessed you'd be head over heels with excitement this morning!'

Ellie landed with a jolt and spun round at the sound of the familiar voice. Her gym coach, Fran, was standing outside the little boathouse watching her with a smile playing across her lips.

'Fran!' Ellie cried. 'What are you doing here?'

'Your dad said this is where I'd find you,' Fran laughed. 'And I couldn't let you go without saying goodbye, could I?'

'Thank you,' Ellie said, still breathless. 'For coming to see me off. And . . . for everything. I couldn't have done it without you.'

Fran sat down on a rock and Ellie perched next to her. Fran hardly looked old enough to be a coach. With her small, compact gymnast's body, rosy face and long, dark hair, she could have been mistaken for Ellie's older sister. She had been coaching Ellie since Ellie was a little girl of five. She'd been the one who first picked her for the Beginner's squad, seeing some spark of talent in her all those years ago. Since then she'd witnessed Ellie's triumphs – and

3

her failures; seen her battling competition nerves, injuries and setbacks; seen the way she pushed herself harder, determined to be the best.

And it had been Fran who'd suggested the move to the Academy. She'd always said she didn't want to push Ellie too fast, that a careful and steady approach was best. But last month she'd told Ellie that if she wanted to go all the way – to British Championships, Worlds, maybe even the Olympics – she would need to move to a bigger club. And of course that's what Ellie wanted! It was all she had ever dreamed of since she was a little girl.

Fran had asked her old friend Emma Bannerdown, former World Champion and now director of the London Gymnastics Academy, to give Ellie a trial. To Ellie's astonishment, Emma had agreed. And, to her even greater amazement, she'd offered Ellie a scholarship to train at the Academy.

All this had happened in the last few dizzying weeks, and Ellie could still barely believe it was true.

'You know you'll be behind the other girls there,' said Fran. 'It could be tough trying to catch up.'

Ellie nodded, feeling butterflies dance in her stomach.

'Maybe I was wrong to hold you back.' Fran looked more serious now. 'I don't know. But, whatever happens, there's something I want you to remember.'

'What's that?' Ellie looked up at her coach eagerly.

'Well, there are three kinds of gymnasts,' said Fran. 'There are power gymnasts – all muscles and strength. There are technical gymnasts, capable of executing moves with an incredible degree of difficulty. And then there are the artistic gymnasts.' She smiled. 'Artistic gymnasts perform with their heart. Think of Nadia Comăneci, Sian Edwards – your Aunt Lizzie. When each of those gymnasts steps on to the floor, she tells a story. They are breathtaking to watch, not just because of the skill they exhibit, but because they turn gym from a sport into an art.'

Ellie thought of the footage she'd watched of her aunt, springing across the blue floor at World

5

Championships. She really looked as if she was dancing over the creek, her arms moving like the swaying of the trees.

'I think you have the soul of an artistic gymnast, Ellie,' Fran said with a smile. 'Remember that. You have strength too – from all the rowing and sailing you do. And wonderful poise – although you need to improve your balance on the beam . . .'

Ellie nodded. She knew the beam was her weakest piece of apparatus.

'But most of all you have heart.'

Ellie felt as if her heart might actually burst. Fran expected a lot of her gymnasts, so compliments from her really meant something.

'So it doesn't matter that you're behind the other girls at the Academy,' Fran was going on. 'Stay true to who you are and who knows how far you can go.'

'But how do I do that?' asked Ellie.

'Hang on to all this,' said Fran, gesturing around her at the little sandy beach, the boathouse, the wooden pontoon stretching out into the lapping waves. 'The creek is part of you. Don't let it go.'

CHAPTER
Two

'There you are! I've been looking for you everywhere!'

Ellie turned to see her little sister come flying down on to the beach, bouncing across the sand. She came to a breathless stop by Ellie and Fran.

'I told Mum you'd be here,' Lucy squeaked excitedly. 'She says you need to get a move on or you'll miss the train. Ooh – did you say goodbye to *Jorian*? And *Diablo*? And little *Roo*?'

Ellie grinned. 'Not yet, no.'

Lucy frowned and put her hands on her hips. Ten years old, with wild red hair and a rosy face full of freckles and dimples, Lucy looked nothing like pale, sandy-haired Ellie who was three years older than her. People sometimes refused to believe they were sisters – until they noticed their eyes, which were the exact same shade of cornflower blue, framed with startling black lashes.

'Well, you need to. They're going to miss you,' Lucy insisted. 'But I'm going to look after *Jorian*. I'll take her out every single day for you, keep her in good condition.'

The way Lucy spoke, you'd have thought she was talking about her pet dog or horse. But *Jorian* was Ellie's old rowing boat. Living on the creek, both girls had learned to row pretty much as soon as they could walk. Dad was a boat-builder, so for Ellie's seventh birthday he'd made her a beautiful ten-foot dinghy from salvaged wood, painted blue and white. She couldn't imagine a day going by without going out in *Jorian*, with Lucy beside her in her boat, *Roo*.

'And *I'm* going to miss you too,' said Lucy, her bright face filled suddenly with sadness. 'But I've decided I'm going to work really hard at gym so I can come to the Academy one day. Aren't I, Fran?'

'So you keep telling me,' said Fran, who had a soft spot for Ellie's crazy sister. Then she glanced at her watch. 'But I think you should get going, Ellie. You don't want to miss that train.'

'Ooh, no,' said Lucy, slipping her hand in Ellie's and tugging her up towards the cottage. 'You can't be late for your first day at the Academy!'

Ellie took one last look around. She'd grown up on the creek, spent every day of her life messing around on the water, rowing, crabbing, collecting shells with Lucy, helping Dad in the boatyard or Mum in her painting studio. She tried to drink it all in, as if she could carry it with her – just like Fran had said. Then she turned and made her way back up to the cottage.

'Darling, I'm so sorry we can't come up to London with you,' Mum was saying as she darted around the kitchen searching for her mobile phone and her car keys. 'This exhibition is so important. If I could sell a few more paintings it would make all the difference. You know.'

'I know, Mum,' said Ellie. 'Sending me to the Academy is expensive.'

'Oh it's not that. You've done so well to get this scholarship,' said Mum. 'There's just a lot of other things to get – what with uniform for your new school – and all the things you'll need because of transferring in the middle of the year . . .'

Ellie's stomach did a flip and she stopped listening for a moment. She'd almost forgotten she was starting at a new school. She'd been so focused on the new gym she hadn't given it much thought.

'Of course we'll muddle through like we always do,' Mum was saying. 'It's just . . .'

'I understand,' said Ellie. It wasn't that they were poor exactly. Dad had always made enough to get by with his boat building and Mum's paintings sold well to tourists in the summer months, but gymnastics was an expensive sport and, though they never said so, Ellie knew they'd already given up a lot to help her follow her dream.

'And the train fares, you know,' Mum went on, still searching for her mobile phone. 'It's astonishing how much it costs for a return ticket these days.'

Next to her two petite daughters, Mum seemed like a giant – and a very strange giant at that! She was nearly six feet tall with a cloud of frizzy red hair and an extremely odd dress sense. Today, she was wearing an orange tie-dye kaftan with green patent boots and what looked like a feather boa wrapped round her waist. She had a paintbrush stuck in her hair, which was spattered with tiny blobs of coloured paint.

'Looking for this?' asked Lucy, pulling Mum's ancient phone from out of the fruit bowl.

'Of course. I knew I'd put it somewhere safe!'

Ellie grinned at Lucy. They were used to finding their school books in the dishwasher, or Mum blowing up the microwave because she'd accidentally tried to nuke her car keys.

'Now. Where's your dad?' Mum said, squinting as if she might find him hiding in the fruit bowl too.

'I bet he's down at the boatyard,' said Ellie. 'He's probably totally forgotten I'm leaving today.'

'Would I ever do a thing like that?' said Dad,

appearing at the back door, wearing a faded fisherman's jumper and a chauffeur's cap covered in sawdust. It was easy to see where Ellie got her looks from – Dad was small and wiry with sandy hair and eyes the colour of the sea. 'Your carriage awaits, Gymnastic Princess,' he said with a flourish of his cap.

'What on earth are you wearing, Dad?' giggled Lucy.

'The Landrover's on the blink again,' Dad said, then bowed low and declared, 'So *Diablo* begs the privilege of escorting Britain's next great gymnastic champion to the station!'

'What?' shrieked Lucy. 'We're going by boat?'

'What could be more appropriate,' said Dad. 'Tide's perfect and it's not too choppy. It's far quicker than the coast road anyway.'

Lucy jumped up and down excitedly and Ellie couldn't help smiling. One last trip out on the water before she left the creek. What better way to say goodbye?

CHAPTER
Three

They arrived at the station with just minutes to spare. There was only time for some hasty hugs on the platform and Lucy pushed a package into Ellie's hands. 'Just a little good-luck present from me,' she said shyly. 'Open it on the train.'

'Thanks, Lucy!' said Ellie, touched by her sister's kindness and realising how desperately she was going to miss her.

Just then the guard blew his whistle and Ellie jumped on board as he yelled at Lucy to stand clear.

'We'll email you – and Face-thingie – and Twittle – and all that stuff!' shouted Mum as the train started to draw away from the platform.

Ellie leaned out of the window to wave. 'But you don't know how to do any of those things!' she laughed.

'Don't worry, I'll show them!' said Lucy.

'Good! Oh – and don't let Dad blow up the boat-shed,' shouted Ellie. 'Or let Mum paint the cat blue – or try to feed you watercolour soup . . .'

'That was an accident!' cried Mum.

'I'll be home at half term!' called Ellie. But the train was gaining speed and her final words were blown away. She could just see Lucy, waving like her life depended on it, getting smaller and smaller on the platform.

'Goodbye, Cornwall. London, here I come!' Ellie whispered as the train started on its journey from the seaside home she loved towards a future she'd been dreaming for as long as she could remember.

She stood by the window for ages, watching as the train made its way along a section of track that seemed to skirt right along the edge of the clifftop. Even though it was January, the sun was bright and the sky clear, and Ellie could see the ocean stretched out like the blue practice floor at the gym.

Finally, she turned away from the window, but somehow she couldn't face going into the carriage to sit with the crowds of people, so she plonked herself down on her suitcase by the bike racks and unwrapped Lucy's gift. She gasped as she lifted the tissue paper to reveal a beautiful new leotard – all silvers and greens and blues – the colours of the ocean, Ellie thought. It was so beautiful, and it was so sweet of Lucy – who must have been saving her pocket money for ages – that she felt suddenly like crying.

Determined not to let the tears come, she folded the leotard carefully into her rucksack then tugged out her favourite gymnastics book and opened it on a well-thumbed page. This book always made her smile. There was a picture of a young gymnast doing a backwards walkover on the beam. She made it look so easy and yet Ellie remembered her own struggles to achieve that move.

There was another picture on the opposite

page of the same gymnast performing a floor routine. The photographer had caught her mid split-leap and she looked almost as if she was flying. Her face was focused, but also serene – as if she was feeling the moves as well as executing them. Wasn't that what Fran had said Ellie should try to do?

The young gymnast's face was as familiar to Ellie as her own – which was hardly surprising since it was almost like looking in a mirror. The girl must have been about sixteen when that picture was taken – just three years older than Ellie – and she shared Ellie's pale brown hair and her large expressive blue eyes.

There were other pictures on the page too. Of the same gymnast holding aloft a trophy at the British Championships, aged just fifteen. Of her performing a gold-medal-winning vault at World Champs two years later. With her teammates on the way to the Olympics, hope shining on their faces. Underneath the last picture a caption read, *Britain's top gymnast, Lizzie Trengilly, just before the tragic fall that ended her career.*

A shiver went down Ellie's spine as she took in the page for what must have been the millionth time. It always thrilled her to think that she was actually related to the great Lizzie Trengilly.

Today, more than ever, she wished she could talk to Lizzie about her time at the Academy. But Lizzie had turned her back completely on gymnastics after that terrible injury. She'd always been a bit of a free spirit, so she'd taken off round the world – teaching sport to street kids in South America, helping save gorillas in the African jungle and who knew what else. Ellie wasn't sure if Aunt Lizzie even knew she was going to the Academy.

Ellie sighed. Maybe one day she could talk to her about all this. Until then she had to keep working hard, and try to achieve her greatest ambition – the one she'd never shared with anyone – to fulfil Aunt Lizzie's dream of Olympic gold.

Dreams of Olympic glory helped Ellie pass the time, but by midday the train was hot and sticky and she was stiff and ravenous. She munched on the strange sandwiches her mum had made for her – peanut butter and smoked salmon sprinkled with popping candy – as the train rumbled through fields and villages on its journey towards London.

'Tickets, please.'

The guard was standing over Ellie with a kindly expression on his face. She rummaged around in her bag and handed him the ticket.

'Now, I'm curious,' said the guard with a twinkle in his eye. 'How on earth do you manage to sit comfortably in that particular position?'

Ellie looked down and realised she was sitting virtually in the splits, one leg stuck out to the side, the other folded inwards. 'Oh – um – I suppose – I – well, I do a lot of gymnastics.'

'Ah,' said the guard, his face lighting up. 'A gymnast! I thought perhaps you'd dislocated your hips or something, and I was just wondering if I needed to pull the red cord and call for medical help.'

Ellie giggled.

'Off to the Olympics are you, young lady?'

'One day, I hope,' said Ellie.

'Goodness me, a world-famous gymnast on my train!' exclaimed the guard.

Ellie grinned. 'I hope so.'

'Well, take a look out of the window and get your first glimpse of the Big Smoke.'

The guard tugged down the window and Ellie was amazed to see that the fields and villages had been replaced by rows of buildings that stretched as far as the eye could see, red-bricked terraces side by side with glistening office blocks and concrete shopping centres, traffic fumes mingling with neon signs in the cold grey winter's afternoon. The sun had disappeared and it all seemed so different to Cornwall – so gloomy and crowded. Ellie wondered how she would ever feel at home here.

'Newcomers to the city get to make a wish,' said the guard.

'Oh,' said Ellie. 'Um – right.' She closed her eyes and made her wish.

'Let's hope London makes all your dreams come true,' said the guard with a grin. Ellie shivered, but she wasn't sure if it was excitement, cold or fear.

'Now, I'd best be getting on,' said the guard. 'And no somersaulting down the aisles on my train, y'hear? Or I might have to impose a penalty fare.'

CHAPTER
Four

In no time the train was drawing into Paddington Station and Ellie gathered up her belongings and made her way on to the platform. She took a deep breath to steady her nerves. The concourse was jammed with people and she wasn't sure who she was looking for.

'Ellie! Ellie!' A voice sailed high above the crowd and Ellie turned to see a girl holding up a poster with 'Academy Ellie' painted on it. It was just like she'd seen in the movies, only this poster was massive, glittery and covered in hearts and pictures of gymnasts. Ellie couldn't help smiling.

There was no way she could miss that!

No longer feeling so nervous, Ellie made her way over. The girl had hair the colour of toffee cake, a face like a pixie and an upturned nose covered in freckles. As soon as she caught sight of Ellie, she squealed out, 'It's you! I recognised you right away because you look just like a fairy. All gymnasts are tiny – except me. I'm shooting up like a weed, Tam says. I'm Nancy by the way. Welcome to London!'

'Thanks for coming to meet me,' said Ellie as soon as she managed to get a word in. 'I love the sign.'

'We've been dead excited about you coming,' Nancy went on happily. 'Especially me cos we're going to be sharing a room. You might not be so excited after you see what a mess I make, but I'm going to try not to be total nightmare, I promise . . .'

Ellie laughed. Nancy's giddy excitement reminded her of Lucy and made her feel at home right away.

'Nancy, let the poor girl get her breath,' laughed a willowy blonde woman who had just reached Nancy's side. She had to be Nancy's mum, because

22

she looked just like her, only her eyes had a kind light that was softer than Nancy's mischievous twinkle.

'Yeah, like that's gonna happen!' said a boy who had appeared apparently from nowhere. He had dark unruly hair and chocolate-brown eyes that sparkled as he grinned at Ellie. Despite the difference in colouring (and the fact that he was a boy) he bore such a startling resemblance to Nancy it was kind of weird looking at the two of them side by side. 'The only time my sis ever stops is when she's asleep – and sometimes not even then. You'll be lucky if you get a wink of sleep sharing a room with Nance! She can talk for England.'

'Oi! Shut up, Tam!' said Nancy, punching the boy on the arm.

'Trust me, I know what I'm talking about,' Tam went on, ignoring her. 'I had to share Mum's tummy with her for a whole nine months. It's a miracle I ever made it out alive.'

Ellie smiled. So they were twins. And, despite the glare that Nancy shot at her brother, Ellie could tell

23

that there was a bond between them like the one she felt with Lucy.

'If you two have finished bickering, shall we do some proper introductions?' said the twins' mum. 'I'm Mandy and these are my troublesome twins, Tam and Nancy.'

'At your service,' said Tam, bending low in a way that made Nancy giggle.

'Tam?' said Ellie. 'I've never heard that name before.'

'Short for Tamar. Apparently I'm named after some river near where Mum and Dad went for honeymoon or something.'

'Oh yes! It's in Cornwall,' said Ellie. 'At least, it runs between Cornwall and Devon. Haven't you ever been there?'

'Nope,' declared Tam. 'We were born in the city and haven't ventured out much our whole lives.'

'Well, I've never been to London before,' said Ellie. 'So I suppose that makes us sort of – I don't know – opposites?'

'Ooh! Then we'll have to show you all the sights,'

said Nancy. 'Buckingham Palace, Big Ben, the London Eye – the lot!'

'Let's just get Ellie back to Head-Over-Heels House for now,' laughed Mandy. 'She must be exhausted and hungry after her long journey. She probably isn't ready for your magical mystery tour just yet!'

'Head-Over-Heels House?' said Ellie, confused.

'Oh,' Tam said, 'that's the nickname for the shared house where all the out-of-town Academy students live – the girls anyway.'

'Some of the students came up with the nickname years ago and it kind of stuck,' said Mandy. 'It actually suits the place because it's a bit topsy-turvy. You'll see what I mean when we get there.'

'I can't wait!' Ellie bent down to pick up her suitcase, but Tam reached for it at exactly the same time and their heads clashed.

'Ow!' said Ellie, rubbing her forehead.

'Oops! Sorry!' said Tam. 'Just wondered if you needed a hand.'

Nancy giggled. 'She's a gymnast! She's probably got stronger arm muscles than you.'

'Yeah, right!' said Tam. 'All you girl gymnasts do is silly flicky-flacky prancing around stuff. It's us boys who do the real strength disciplines.'

'Is that right?' said Nancy. 'I'd like to see you manage a flick layout on the beam!'

'And you wouldn't last two minutes on the pommel horse,' said Tam with a shrug.

Mandy shook her head and smiled at Ellie. 'They've been having this argument since they started gym when they were four years old.'

'Is this all the stuff you have?' Tam asked, looking round. 'I thought you'd have loads of bags.'

Before Ellie had a chance to think of a reply, Nancy had punched her brother's shoulder again and linked arms with Ellie. 'Don't be stupid. All she needs is a few leotards, her hand guards and a tracksuit,' she said. 'After all, she's going to spend most of her life in the Academy, just like the rest of us. Now, if you could just stop talking for a single moment . . .'

'*Me* stop talking!'

Nancy ignored him. 'Head-Over-Heels House, here we come!'

CHAPTER
Five

They caught a tube and a bus and Ellie was amazed
by how many people there were. On the creek,
you could go all day without seeing anyone. But in
London every square centimetre of space seemed
to be filled with life. People crammed on to the
platform, streaming down the escalators, squeezed
like sardines into the tube carriages and on the
buses. To Ellie, it felt totally insane but brilliantly
exciting at the same time.

'London must seem pretty full on,' said Tam,
noticing her wide eyes. 'You live by the seaside,
right?'

'Sort of,' said Ellie. 'On a little tidal estuary, just inland from the sea.'

'Cool,' said Nancy. 'Do you go surfing every day, and sailing and water-skiing? I've always wanted to try water-skiing. And rowing. I'd love to be able to row.'

'I go rowing most days,' said Ellie. 'I have my own boat that my dad made for me.'

'Awesome!' said Nancy. 'I reckon if I get too tall for gymnastics I'm going to be a rower. They're always pretty tall, aren't they? And I've got strong arms. Scarlett reckons I'm more like a weightlifter than a gymnast – but that's the sort of thing she would say.'

'Um – who's Scarlett?' asked Ellie.

'Oh, she's in Development squad like us,' explained Nancy. 'And she lives in Head-Over-Heels House because her mum and dad are always off travelling overseas. They're like multi-millionaires or something – as she's always reminding everybody.' Nancy rolled her eyes but didn't stop talking. Ellie was starting to wonder how she managed to breathe sometimes. 'Anyway, she reckons she's ten times better than the rest of us in Development squad. She's not going to like you – at all!'

'Oh.' Ellie's face fell. 'Why?'

'Because you've come from nowhere and been given a place at the Academy,' said Tam.

'Most of us've been training there for years,' Nancy explained. 'Tam and I started at the Academy before we even went to school. I mean, sometimes gymnasts come from other big gyms overseas, like Camille – she's half French, half Belgian – or Lily Raza – her parents sent her all the way from Israel just to train with Emma. But people don't usually just get picked from little tiny clubs. There must be something special about you for Emma to take you on.'

Ellie blushed, finding it hard to believe. The bus was going over a bridge and Ellie caught a glimpse of the River Thames, crowded with city vessels, the water dark and oily in the falling dusk. It was so different to the creek, but still somehow the sight of it reminded her of home.

'I don't know,' she said. 'I mean, I think I'm way behind the rest of you. I don't have my Compulsory Grade Two yet.'

'Oh, me neither,' said Nancy. 'I've failed it twice now.' She shrugged like it was no big deal, but there was something in her face that made Ellie think she was more bothered than she was letting on.

'Got to get it this time or I won't be able to go to British Champs,' Nancy went on. 'We're old enough to compete at the Junior British this year. But I guess you know that. Of course, Scarlett passed every grade first time so she'll be going for Grade One this year. And Camille and Kashvi and Bella are too. They're the other girls in Development. They're all cool – it's only Scarlett who thinks she's too good for the rest of us. But if she *was* so good Emma would have promoted her to Pre-Elite squad, so I don't know why she's strutting around, pretending she's Lizzie Trengilly or something.'

Ellie blushed again at the mention of her aunt. She wasn't sure if Nancy or anyone else at the Academy knew that she was related to the famous gymnast. Nancy's sign had just said 'Academy Ellie' – so maybe they didn't even know her second name. Ellie was almost relieved. It wasn't that she wanted to keep it a secret, but she didn't want to go around boasting either.

'Seriously, though, you need to watch out for Scarlett,' said Tam. 'That girl is determined to get to the top, no matter what it takes.'

'Yup,' Nancy agreed. 'She'll be nice to you as long as she doesn't think you're a threat. But if she decides you might have a chance of being better than her one day then . . .'

Just at that moment the bus lurched to a stop, sending Ellie flying into Nancy, who had toppled into the doorway.

'Here we are!' said Tam, 'This is our stop.'

Head-Over-Heels House turned out to be a big, old Victorian house on Albert Bridge Road, overlooking Battersea Park. It had probably once been quite grand, but now it looked pretty scruffy. The door was painted bright purple and somebody had made a sign that read 'Head-Over-Heels House' with a picture of a gymnast doing a backwards walkover.

Being opposite the park made the house feel less hemmed in by the city, and to Ellie's delight she noticed that they were still close to the river. The smell of the Thames hung in the air and again it reminded her of the creek.

'Come on in,' said Nancy, flinging open the door. 'Welcome to the madhouse!'

'It's huge!' said Ellie as she stepped into a giant hallway with a swooping staircase, faded marble tiles and battered wallpaper.

'Well, there are six other gymnasts living here,' Mandy explained. 'All out-of-towners like you. And then my two, of course.'

'Mum can't get enough gymnasts to look after, can you, Mum?' said Tam.

'And none of them are half as much trouble as you two,' laughed Mandy, ruffling Tam's hair. 'But, seriously, Ellie, here in Head-Over-Heels House we're all family. I want you to think of me as someone you can always come to. If you have any problems – no matter how big or small – my door is always open. OK?'

'Thanks,' said Ellie.

'Come on, I'll show you our room,' said Nancy, dashing up the staircase.

Ellie followed her, half in a daze, trying to take it all in.

'There are a couple of other Development squad girls here,' said Nancy, calling over her shoulder. 'Then there are two from Junior Elite and one Pre-Elite girl. No boys, except for Tam, but he's in the basement with Mum. Oh, and Sian Edwards and Sophia Mitford share the attic flat. They're both Senior Elite, of course.'

'Sian Edwards – the Olympian?' said Ellie, amazed. She'd watched Sian compete for Team GB at World Championships last year, and been dazzled by her amazing performance on the vault, which had helped to earn her a gold medal. 'She lives here – in this house?'

'Well, in the flat upstairs,' said Nancy, like it was no big deal. 'She's dead nice. Never too busy to chat to any of us kids in Development squad either.'

Ellie couldn't imagine what she'd do if she bumped into Sian Edwards over breakfast, or in her pyjamas. The idea of chatting to a gold-medal-winning Olympian seemed too crazy.

'So, this is our pad,' Nancy was saying as she opened the door to a room on the second floor and ushered Ellie in. The room was tiny and had a slightly tatty appearance like the rest of the house, but it had a large window overlooking the garden and a beautiful old fireplace in the corner.

On Nancy's side, the walls were covered in posters of gymnasts and boy bands and kittens dressed in a variety of weird and wonderful costumes – including one in a sparkly pink leotard. Her bed and every surface was strewn with leotards and scrunchies and jogging bottoms.

On Ellie's side was a bed with a patchwork quilt, a small chest of drawers and a massive bouquet of flowers in a chipped vase. There were also a couple of framed pictures. One was a painting of a beach in Cornwall which Ellie recognised as

35

Kynance Cove, not far from the creek. The other was a photo of a gymnast on the uneven bars, mid twist, her body swooping like a seagull into the dive. Ellie knew who it was immediately and her heart leapt.

'D'you like the Cornwall painting?' asked Nancy. 'Tam found it in a charity shop. He reckoned it would be perfect, in case you felt homesick for the beach, you know. I did the flowers.'

Ellie looked at the colourful blooms – huge gaudy pinks, oranges and even blue flowers. 'Thank you. They're lovely!' she said, touched by the thought.

Nancy smiled brightly. 'Tam figured you'd like the photo too – since you're family, an' all.'

'Oh, so you know, then,' said Ellie nervously. 'About Lizzie Trengilly . . . being my aunt.'

'Of course!' chirped Nancy. 'I mean, no offence, but it didn't exactly take major detective work. The name Trengilly isn't that common, is it? And the minute we saw your picture we knew right away. You look just like her. I bet you're as good as she was too,' Nancy went on, flinging herself on to her bed amidst all the muddle. 'I've got a feeling about it, looking at you.'

'How can you tell if I'm any good at gym just by looking at me?'

'I dunno,' said Nancy. 'But I can. Maybe I'm psychic – Tam reckons I'm a bit weird like that, y'know. But I bet you anything I'm right!'

CHAPTER
Six

Just then there was a knock on the door and Ellie turned to see a face peeping into the room.

'Can we come in?'

The door creaked open to reveal a tiny girl with a round face, big velvety dark eyes and sticky-out ears. The little buns she wore on each side of her head made her look a bit like a baby monkey. She was standing next to a taller girl with golden hair, a flawless complexion and green cat-like eyes.

'Bella! Scarlett!' squeaked Nancy, jumping off the bed. 'Meet Ellie, my new roomie and our new squad buddy. Ellie, meet the Floor Fairy, Bella Chee and Queen of the Beam, Scarlett Atkins.'

Bella smiled broadly and said in a soft voice, 'Welcome to Head-Over-Heels House.'

But Scarlett narrowed her eyes and said, 'Is it true Emma gave you a scholarship even though you haven't even passed Compulsory Grade Two yet?'

'Scarlett, don't put her on the spot,' said Bella. She spoke with a gentle authority, despite being so small she even made Ellie look like a giant.

'It's OK,' said Ellie. 'Scarlett's right. I didn't start Compulsory Grades till I was quite old. My coach didn't think I was ready.'

'I passed Grade Two when I was eleven.' Ambition flared in Scarlett's eyes as she spoke. 'I won the bronze medal. Because you do know that Grades are also a competition, right?'

'Um – yes,' said Ellie.

'Of course she does!' said Nancy.

'Well, I'll be doing Grade One this year. Which is higher than Grade Two – in case you didn't realise.'

'She's from Cornwall!' said Nancy. 'Not a whole different planet.'

'Well, how should I know how they do things in the middle of nowhere?' said Scarlett.

'You might want to remember that Bella won the gold when we did Grade Two,' said Nancy, who looked as if she was keen to prick Scarlett's bubble. 'And all the other girls in Development squad are up for Grade One this year too.'

'Except you, of course,' said Scarlett with a smile. 'Let's hope you get third time lucky with your Grade Two, Nancy, or we'll all be going to the British without you!'

'Stop arguing, you guys!' said Bella firmly. 'Remember what Emma's always saying. We're teammates, not rivals. We perform better if we support each other.'

Scarlett glared and Nancy gave a 'hmmph!' sound. But just then a clamour in the hallway and a call of '*Food!*' signalled that dinner was ready, and all arguments were set aside as they raced downstairs to eat.

'Is that true?' Nancy whispered, linking arms with Ellie as the girls made their way down the stairs.

'About you having a scholarship.'

'Um – yeah.' Ellie flushed, suddenly embarrassed. 'My parents couldn't afford for me to train here otherwise.'

Nancy shrugged. 'Yeah, well, we can only afford it cos of Mum – you know, being Head-Over-Heels house-mother, or whatever you call it. But, seriously, the Academy hardly ever give out scholarships. Emma must think you're really good.'

'I dunno . . .' Ellie started to say.

'I wonder how Scarlett found out?' Nancy was musing as she pulled open the door to the kitchen.

Sitting round the giant dining table, Ellie met most of the other residents of the house. She thought she'd be too nervous to eat, but after the long journey and all the excitement she was starving so she tucked in to the biggest dish of shepherd's pie she'd ever seen in her life.

Nancy and Bella introduced her to the others. Isobel Mallin and Mia Rudolph from Junior Elite squad made a funny pair. Isabel was tall, quiet and serious-looking, whilst Mia was small and a total chatterbox – but they were clearly the best of friends.

Then there was Bree Summers from Pre-Elite who told lots of funny stories about her squad coach, Oleg Petrescu. There was no sign of Sian Edwards or Sophia Mitford, and Nancy told Ellie they had been off at a Team GB training weekend and would be back tomorrow.

Ellie tried to imagine that one day she might be picked for Team GB, but right now it was enough to be here, an Academy girl – or very nearly anyway.

'I thought Oleg was going to explode today,' Bree was saying, 'when Lily kept sneezing and couldn't stop.'

The other girls all giggled and Nancy turned to Ellie to explain. 'Oleg Petrescu is Romanian, and basically a living legend! One of the seven ancient wonders of the gymnastics world.'

'He looks like a tiny little weightlifter and he's got this giant moustache – all curly like a circus ringmaster or something,' added Mia with a giggle.

'And he's got a thing about germs and people being ill,' Bella explained. 'Remember when Pearl had mumps and he acted like she had the plague?'

'Yeah, and I basically spent the whole year I was in Pre-Elite terrified of even getting a headache,' Isobel said with a frown.

'Anyway, when Lily sneezed for the tenth time, Oleg started screaming like a bomb had gone off and kicked her out of the gym,' Bree went on.

'No – he sent her out?'

'Right away,' said Bree. 'Then he started spraying the vault with anti-bacterial spray. And you should have seen the masks he got out of his bag. Like nurses wear. He wanted all of us in Pre-Elite to wear them so we didn't catch anything.'

'What did Emma say?' asked Nancy.

'Oh, Emma knows Oleg's funny ways, but she also knows he's the best vault coach in the world,' said Bree with a shrug. 'Oleg was going on about the English weather and going to California where it was sunny all day, so Emma said she'd arrange for everyone in the gym to have multi-vitamins and loads of oranges to make sure we get don't get colds.'

'What did he say to that?' said Mia.

'He went off into a flurry of Romanian and flung his arms around a bit – you know how he does,' said Bree, doing an impression of Oleg, which made everyone laugh again. 'But he let Lily come back into training – and he was so sweet and apologetic. He made her a lemon-and-honey drink and everything.'

'He really is a total sweetie, isn't he?' said Bella.

'He's lovely!' said Bree. 'He gets so upset with himself for losing his temper, and then he fusses over you like anything. Lily will get the royal treatment for at least a week.'

'Not like Toni,' said Nancy, rolling her eyes. 'When Toni's annoyed, he goes totally silent. The quieter he is the more you know you're doing it wrong.'

'Toni Nimakov, you know,' Bella explained, turning to Ellie who was tucking into her second helping of shepherd's pie.

'Don't be stupid!' said Scarlett, who hadn't said much up to this point. 'Of course Ellie's heard of Toni Nimakov. He's won four Olympic gold medals, he coached Emma Bannerdown and Lizzie

Trengilly. Even girls from tiny gym clubs in Devon must know that.'

'Cornwall,' said Ellie quietly.

'What?'

'My gym club is in Cornwall,' Ellie repeated. 'And, yes, I have heard of Toni Nimakov, but I thought he only coached the Elite squads.'

'Oh, he does, but sometimes he comes and helps us with our bar work,' said Nancy, shooting Scarlett a look. 'Which is terrifying because he picks up on the teensiest faults.'

'And if you actually do it right, he might manage two words of praise,' said Mia with a rueful grin.

'Yes, but two words from Toni can put you on top of the world,' said Bella, and all the other girls nodded in agreement.

'And he always knows exactly what to say to help you get a move right too,' Isobel said. 'I struggled with the double pike tuck for months and then he came along and in two days he had me getting it every time. I don't even fully remember what he said or did. It's like he's the magic man of the bar.'

45

'What's Sasha like?' Ellie asked. Nancy had told her earlier that Sasha Darling coached the Development squad.

'Oh, Sasha's hilarious,' said Tam, emerging from the kitchen with a tray of apple crumble and a steaming jug of creamy custard. He might be the only boy in Head-Over-Heels House, but he certainly didn't seem intimidated by all the girls. 'Did you know she won Junior British Champs when she was fourteen, and Senior the following year, then she gave it all up to go to Hollywood and work in the movies?'

'Really?' said Ellie.

'Oh, yes. She played Nadia Comăneci in a film,' said Nancy. 'Then she worked in Las Vegas in an acrobatics circus show and she was in an American TV series, and all sorts.'

'When Emma took over at the Academy she begged Sasha to come and coach,' Tam added, plonking the crumble and custard down on the table and stepping back as all the gymnasts dived in at once.

'Emma reckoned Sasha was born to be a coach, and she was right,' said Bella. 'She's awesome. But don't be fooled by all her pink sparkle and fun, cos she can be really strict if she thinks you're messing around.'

'I reckon she's the strictest coach of them all,' said Nancy, helping herself to a giant plate of dessert. 'She'll make you work over and over and over on a move until you get it right.'

'But when you do she gives you a hug,' said Bella with a grin. 'And I can't imagine any of the other coaches doing that, can you?'

'If Oleg tried to hug you, he'd probably crush you to death!' laughed Bree. 'And Toni looks like he's never given anyone a cuddle in his life.'

'As for Emma, she'll only give you a hug when you win Olympic gold,' added Nancy. The table fell silent for a moment, as every gymnast there imagined standing on the podium at the Olympics with a gold medal round their necks. Then Nancy laughed and added, 'Which means never in my case!'

CHAPTER
Seven

Ellie didn't think she'd be able to sleep with the sound of the city humming around her. She was so used to the silence and pitch black of the creek nights, and couldn't get used to the traffic and sirens, and even once the thrum of a helicopter flying low overhead. But she drifted off far more quickly than she expected to, and dreamed of doing round-off flicks along the tube platform and vaulting over Albert Bridge.

She woke up the next morning feeling surprisingly refreshed, although by the time she got down for breakfast the butterflies in her stomach felt as if they were doing an energetic floor routine. She found it almost impossible to force anything down, even though Mandy's pancakes and scrambled eggs were every bit as delicious as last night's dinner had been.

'So, did you manage to sleep through Nancy's bulldozer snoring?' was the first thing Tam asked when he appeared for breakfast.

'I do not snore!' said Nancy.

'Yeah, right! And I suppose you reckon you don't talk in your sleep either!' said Tam. 'Seriously, you spend all night muttering about how I'm a far better gymnast than you are.'

'Then I'm an even bigger liar in my sleep than you are in the daytime,' Nancy said, quick as a flash.

'Don't you know people always tell the truth in their dreams?' said Tam.

Ellie listened to the good-natured banter, but it didn't quite take her mind off her nerves.

'Come on,' said Nancy, bolting down the last of her pancake. 'We'd better get to the Academy. Can't have you being late on your first day.'

Ellie jumped up as if she'd been scalded. 'Are we late?'

'Actually, no,' said Nancy. 'Which is surprising for me, but I thought I'd make a special effort today since you're new. So, have you got everything? Weights – guards – leo – fluffy socks.'

'Socks?'

'The gym floor is ice cold first thing in the morning. Especially this time of year,' Bella explained, pulling on a coat that looked about two sizes too big for her. 'I can lend you a pair if you haven't got any.'

'Thanks,' said Ellie, as the girls headed off to the front door. How many other Academy traditions would there be to get used to, she wondered. She could hardly wait to find out.

The Academy was only a short walk from Head-Over-Heels House, across the frost-covered park, over a busy road and through some winding backstreets. The other girls had gone on ahead after Nancy had realised she'd forgotten her weights, but Ellie and

Tam had waited for her. It wasn't even 6 a.m. and it was still dark outside, but Ellie was amazed how many people were up and about.

'London never sleeps, Mum reckons,' said Nancy as they ducked past a twenty-four-hour grocery shop and down an alleyway into a courtyard of converted warehouses. And then Ellie found herself standing in front of a battered metal door, above which a sign read 'London Gymnastics Academy – Home of Sian Edwards and Matt Simmons – World Champions!'

Ellie took a deep breath and made a vow to remember this moment. But then a couple of boys – members of the boys' squad, she guessed – nearly knocked her off her feet as they raced up the steps.

'Right, I'm this way,' said Tam, following the other boys through a large metal door to the left. 'See you later.'

'The boys train in a separate gym next door,' Nancy explained as she led the way to the girls' changing room. 'So you won't have Tam showing off on the rings – which he is annoyingly good at. Don't tell him I said that, though, or I'll have to kill you.'

'Um – no, I won't,' murmured Ellie, standing in the middle of the changing room, staring around half in a daze.

'You're busy thinking about all the famous gymnasts who've got changed here, aren't you?' said Nancy as she plonked down her bag and started tugging off her trainers.

'Um – yes, I was,' said Ellie. 'How did you know?'

'You're one of those romantic types,' said Nancy with a grin. 'I could see that right away. I wish I was like that, only Tam says I have less imagination than a slug. Although slugs could be very imaginative for all he knows.'

Ellie giggled.

'That's rubbish, anyway! You've got the craziest imagination of anyone I know, Nancy!' said Bella who was already in her leotard and pulling on a pair of fluffy socks.

'Yes, the sort of imagination that gets me in trouble for daydreaming, not the kind that makes a world champ,' said Nancy.

'You see, Emma's got this theory that there are

three kinds of gymnasts,' Bella explained, twisting her hair up into two little buns. 'Power gymnasts, technical gymnasts and artistic gymnasts.'

'Oh!' said Ellie. 'That's what my coach Fran said too.' But of course that made sense. Emma and Fran had trained together and competed for Team GB together too – along with Aunt Lizzie.

'According to Emma, you need all three to make it to the top,' said Nancy. 'So, if you've got strength and precision to go with that imagination of yours, you'll be winning gold medals before you know it.'

A couple of other girls appeared at that moment, so Ellie didn't have the chance to reply. She was touched by Nancy's faith in her, but she couldn't help worrying that she wasn't going to live up to anyone's expectations – not even her own.

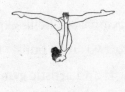

CHAPTER
Eight

The training area wasn't much bigger than the one at Ellie's Cornish gym and every available space was crammed with equipment. Over in the pit, she saw the Pre-Elite squad on bars, whilst the Junior Elite girls were on beam and the Senior Elite were vaulting. Apart from the fact that everyone was doing more advanced moves, it felt a lot like being back home.

Nancy tugged Ellie over to the blue practice floor where the other members of Development squad were already lined up in front of the mirrors. Nancy introduced her to Kashvi Khan who looked like an Indian princess (Ellie found out later that her great-great-great-something had been a maharaja) and Camille Bertinet who looked like a girl from a magazine and was wearing the most gorgeous leotard Ellie had ever seen in her life. Along with Bella, Scarlett, Nancy and herself, they made up the Development squad.

Lining up with them, Ellie caught sight of her own reflection. Under the neon strip lights, she looked pale and much younger than her thirteen years. Despite the fact that she was super strong from all the sailing and rowing, her body looked as breakable as a twig in the new silver and blue training leotard that Lucy had given her. Ellie didn't think she looked like a future champion. What if she wasn't even good enough to cut it at the Academy? She felt a shiver of fear run down her spine.

Academy head coach, Emma Bannerdown, came over to talk to the girls. Ellie had met her only once before – at her trial. Next to her was Sasha Darling, whom she recognised from Nancy's description last night. Looking at them, Ellie couldn't help thinking that the two coaches couldn't have been more different.

Emma had a boyish figure, cropped blonde hair and piercing grey eyes that seemed to see right inside you. Sasha was shorter – tiny in fact – with laughing eyes, bright pink lipstick that matched her tracksuit, and a chestnut-coloured ponytail. She looked a bit like a miniature brunette Barbie doll, and it was easy to see how she'd been a movie star.

'Good morning, cupcakes,' said Sasha brightly. 'As you can see, our great leader, Emma, has come to have a few words with you, so listen up!'

'Emma doesn't normally take too much notice of us,' Nancy whispered to Ellie. 'It must be in your honour.'

'Good morning, girls,' Emma said, her voice crisp and businesslike. 'As you can see, we have a new member of Development squad, and I hope you'll make her feel very welcome.' Ellie wondered if Emma's gaze rested a little longer on Scarlett as she said this, but she couldn't be sure.

'I remind you of what I have said many times

before: that we are a team here at the Academy,' said Emma.

'There's no "I" in squad,' added Sasha cheerily, her ponytail bouncing as she spoke. 'Or in "gym" either – unless you spell it wrong, that is!' she giggled.

'You will all need to work incredibly hard over the next few weeks for Compulsory Grades,' Emma went on, unsmiling. 'Especially those of you who still don't have your Grade Two. Anyone who wants to make it to the British needs to pass so there can be no slacking.'

Ellie's heart did a somersault. Junior British Championships was the most important event in the gymnastics calendar – where the best young gymnasts from all over the country battled it out to be crowned Junior British Champion. From there you could progress to Senior British Champs or even be picked for the GB team to represent your country on the international stage. But you were only eligible to compete at the Championship events if you had passed Compulsory Grade Two.

'But remember that Grades are more than just an exam,' Emma went on. 'It's a competition too – and the top-ranked gymnasts at Grades go into the British with a huge advantage. So, you all need to improve your execution scores and some of you –' this time her eyes seemed to rest on Nancy – 'still have to master the basic range and conditioning exercises.'

'What did I tell you? She sees everything!' whispered Nancy.

'Sasha will be pushing you to your limits,' Emma went on, flashing a warning glance at Nancy, which made Ellie think she probably *heard* everything too. 'Each of you is here because we've seen some potential in you. But potential is nothing without hard work and commitment. Gymnastics is like no other sport – it demands absolute dedication from athletes whilst they are still very young.'

Emma paused and looked the young gymnasts up and down. 'Many find they lack the maturity, the discipline – the hunger to pursue that dream,' she said. 'Others will find their bodies change

– they grow too tall, lose their flexibility – an extra inch of growth can throw a gymnast off her game completely. There will be injuries, setbacks, obstacles and heartbreak. I cannot guarantee any of you standing here will make it. You are giving up a great deal and for many of you there will be no Olympic podium as reward.'

Ellie felt in that moment as if the whole of the rest of the gym disappeared and Emma was speaking to her and her alone.

'But, if you work hard, throw your heart and soul into gymnastics, you will never look back with regret,' Emma went on. 'Gymnastics will teach you discipline and teamwork. It will give you courage and self-belief. You will only get out of this gym what you bring to it, so never walk away wishing you had given more.'

Ellie's heart swelled as Emma's speech came to an end and she made a silent promise to herself that no matter what happened, no matter whether she made it or not, she would give her all to the Academy.

'Right, let's get on,' said Emma. 'I know Sasha wants to see you all working hard this morning.'

'I most certainly do!' said Sasha, her voice chirpy in stark contrast to Emma's low tones. 'And I'm feeling fierce today, my little pumpkins, so any slackers had better watch out.' Sasha bared her pink bejewelled claws as she said this, but she beamed at the same time and didn't look remotely fierce.

'Like I said last night, don't be fooled,' whispered Nancy. 'I promise you that you do not want to unleash the pink fury! Trust me – I know!'

As the girls walked away, Emma called Ellie back. 'It's good to have you at the Academy, Ellie,' she said, looking her up and down with her cool grey eyes.

'I'm really excited to be here.'

'You're a bit behind some of the others so you're going to have to work really hard if you want to catch up. Are you ready for that?'

Ellie nodded.

'Good.' Emma smiled. 'Sasha's a great coach. I think you and she will get on really well together. I look forward to watching your progress.'

'Thank you,' said Ellie, 'and –' she hesitated – 'and thank you for giving me a chance.'

Emma narrowed her eyes and said nothing for a second, then she put her hand on Ellie's shoulder. 'I'm taking a risk on you. Prove to me I was right to take that risk. OK?'

Ellie nodded and for a second she thought Emma looked almost sad, but then her face cleared and she turned away, leaving Ellie to join the rest of her squad for warm-up.

CHAPTER
Nine

That first session in the gym was much harder than Ellie had expected. It was only two hours long, but they worked with far greater intensity than she was used to. And she loved every minute of it.

She was amazed at how talented her squad mates were. Bella was as bendy as a strawberry lace, but incredibly strong and precise. Camille was perfect on the vault, Scarlett breath-taking on the beam, whilst on the floor Kashvi nailed moves Ellie had only ever seen on TV. Poor Nancy didn't seem to be having her best day, wobbling on the beam and missing half her landings on the bar and vault. But she was still more advanced than Ellie. And glancing across the gym to where some of the Senior Elite squad were training made Ellie's head spin. She was obviously the least experienced gymnast there, but strangely that just made her feel excited.

'Wait till Sian and Sophia get back,' whispered Nancy, seeing Ellie gazing over to where Toni was teaching an older girl a new vault. 'They'll blow your mind.'

Surrounded by all this, how could Ellie not be inspired? And Sasha was a brilliant coach. She seemed to be able to weigh up in an instant the tiny adjustments each girl needed to help them improve. In just two hours, she'd shown Ellie a new way of thinking about the layout on the beam that made things so much easier, and she'd helped her complete a new floor move too.

'That's wonderful, my little honeycake!' Sasha cooed when Ellie managed to land the handspring tuck front. 'But do try to look a little less serious. Gymnastics is supposed to be fun!'

And it was fun – amazing in fact – but it was tough

too. On the bar, usually Ellie's strongest apparatus, she was struggling with a straddle catch – a move from the low to the high bar – when she realised that someone was watching her. A small man with an athletic frame and a shaved head was standing a metre or so from the bar with his arms crossed and a frown of concentration on his face.

Ellie recognised him at once: Toni Nimakov, double Olympic Champion and the man who had coached Sian Edwards to Olympic glory. And he was standing there, watching her mess up, over and over again.

Feeling the colour rise in her cheeks, Ellie was determined to show Toni – and herself – that she could do it. But she seemed to get worse and worse until she started to wonder if she could remember how to do anything properly any more. Burning with shame as she fell into the pit for the fourth time in a row, she heard a clear voice say in accented English, 'You need to hold on a little longer before you release. Try again.'

To her amazement, Ellie realised Toni was talking

to her. She hesitated for a second, aware that all the other members of Development – and half the Pre-Elite and Junior Elite girls too – were watching as Toni barked out, 'Again.'

Ellie quickly adjusted her hand guards, which helped her grip the bar, then got herself back into position. This time she would try to hold on to the bar a fraction longer, just as Toni had said. She did the swooping dive, then as she was about to let go she waited and then . . . released. For a second she thought she'd missed the bar then she felt her hands make contact with wood and she realised that she'd done it. That one change had transformed the whole move. As she flung herself into her dismount, Ellie realised why Toni Nimakov was considered the best bar coach in the world.

She looked around nervously, expecting him to have walked away to one of the more senior gymnasts. But he was still there, watching intently. He said nothing for what felt like forever and then, to her surprise, he muttered, 'Nice. Very nice.' Then he turned and hurried off without another word.

Ellie remembered what Bree had said last night. About how any praise – no matter how small – from Toni Nimakov could make you feel on top of the world. Right then, Ellie would have traded every medal she'd ever won for those three little words that had made her feel about six feet tall.

On the other side of the pit, Nancy was grinning and Bella was doing an excited little dance. Ellie flushed with pleasure . . . until she caught sight of Scarlett, who looked as if somebody had just slapped her. She was glaring so hard Ellie felt as if the force of it might topple her over.

And then Ellie remembered what Nancy had said about Scarlett the day before. Had she just made her first enemy at the Academy?

CHAPTER
Ten

Scarlett took every opportunity to have a go at Ellie throughout the rest of the session, criticising her on everything from her splits to her scrunchie. It didn't help that Nancy kept doing impressions of Toni, saying, 'Nice, very nice,' in a terrible Russian accent.

But Ellie felt as if nothing could touch her happiness. By the end of the session she was completely wiped out, but still buzzing.

'You think that was tough. Just wait till you see the stuff they're making us do in maths,' said Nancy, pulling on her crumpled school uniform. 'It makes Sasha's conditioning sessions look like a dream!'

Ellie remembered with a start that she was going to a new school today too. Luckily, Mandy had sorted out uniform for her, otherwise she'd have had to have turned up to class in a leotard and a pair of sweat pants. Mandy had also packed all the Head-Over-Heels House girls a second breakfast – thick crusts of bread and ham, with crispy red apples, all of which Ellie wolfed down greedily.

It was hard to believe it was still only 9 a.m. and just starting to get light outside as she pulled on one of Nancy's old school sweatshirts and a skirt that had been rolled up so often the elastic had gone from the waistband.

'The school's OK,' said Bella. 'And they don't mind us doing reduced hours, which some schools are really funny about.'

'So long as you don't fall behind,' added Nancy, rolling her eyes. 'I failed a single maths test last term and Emma made me miss morning training for a week until I passed my retest. She says all Academy students have to get good grades or the school won't support reduced hours.'

'Well, she's right,' said Scarlett airily. 'Anyway, if you don't have discipline, you'll never make it as a gymnast.'

'It's all very well you saying that,' said Nancy. 'You don't get geometry mixed up with geography, and the only thing I ever get right in history is Olympic dates.'

'How many times have I told you to stop putting yourself down, Nancy?' said Bella. She turned to Ellie and said, 'She likes to make out she's bad at everything – but don't believe a word she says.'

'*Oui!* Nancy, she only pretend to be stoopid for ze laughs!' agreed Camille, who wore her uniform as if it was the latest Parisian chic.

'I wish!' said Nancy. 'I just wish we could study interesting things – like the history of gymnastics. Or if geography was less about capital cities and rivers, and more about famous gymnasts of each country. Then I'd ace it!'

'Yeah, well, nobody will be acing anything if we turn up late,' said Bella. 'So get a move on!'

*

69

Battersea Park Senior School was just on the other side of the river from the Academy – a quick dash across the misty park and then a sprint over the bridge where Ellie just had time to take in the smell of the river as they hurried on their way.

It was a large city comprehensive with three times as many pupils as in Ellie's school back in Cornwall. It felt strange to be starting in the middle of the school year and Ellie was sure she'd never have found her way round it on her own so she was glad to be in the same form as Nancy, Bella and Tam – although she was less delighted when Scarlett appeared too.

'What did you do to annoy the Beam Queen?' asked Tam, noticing the poisonous glare Scarlett shot in Ellie's direction at registration.

'She got a compliment from Toni Nimakov,' Nancy explained.

'Wow,' said Tam, looking impressed. 'Well, that would explain why she looks as if she swallowed a bucketload of gym chalk! You'd better watch your back from now on. She'll have her claws out for you.'

Ellie glanced nervously at Scarlett. She hoped

Tam was exaggerating, but she had a horrible feeling he wasn't.

In her first lesson, the maths teacher, a large flamboyant lady named Miss Trelford, noticed a new name on the register. 'Another Academy student, are you?' she asked. And when Ellie nodded she said, 'Good. You gymnasts are always very focused. Personally, I can't imagine why you want to spend your spare time tying yourself in knots, mind you.'

Nancy giggled and whispered, 'I'm trying to imagine Miss Trelford tying herself in knots!'

'But it obviously teaches you some kind of discipline,' Miss Trelford went on.

Ellie smiled too. Emma had said almost exactly the same thing that morning.

'And why have you transferred in the middle of the school year?' Miss Trelford asked.

'Oh, the gymnastics year runs from January to December, and Ellie just started at the Academy for this year,' Nancy explained before Ellie could get a word in.

'Well, I suppose that makes sense,' said Miss

71

Trelford. 'But, for now, less talk of somersaults and more focus on sums, ladies!'

The first day at school flew by, especially as the Academy pupils were allowed to skip last period on a Monday. Before she knew it, Ellie was on her way back to the gym. This time she and Nancy jumped on a bus to cross the bridge.

'It's pretty manic but you get used to it,' said Nancy as the girls squashed on to the last free seats.

Ellie didn't think it was the schedule she needed to get used to. It was London. She felt as if her senses were being bombarded from every direction – with colours, sounds, smells. She was glad when the bus skirted round the park. The sight of trees and grass and the dog walkers and runners made her feel a bit more at home.

But there was no time to stop and enjoy the view. Soon they had jumped off the bus and hurried into the Academy for a quick change and then back into the gym. The Senior girls were back from the Team GB training camp and Ellie watched wide-eyed as Sian Edwards worked on her famous two and a half twisting Yurchenko vault. The speed of her rotations in the air was amazing. And Sophia Mitford was almost like an ice skater on the beam – she seemed to float there without even a faint trace of a wobble.

The Development squad was focusing on range and conditioning – the compulsory exercises to display strength and flexibility which they had to complete to pass each grade. Once again Ellie found herself behind the others. She was grateful when Sasha said, 'You're doing well and you'll get it. Just keep at it, little munchkin.' But by the time she and the others bundled into the changing room at 8 p.m., Ellie was more tired than she'd ever felt in her life.

It was weird getting changed alongside an Olympic champion, and Ellie was surprised to overhear Sian telling Sophia she had to see Emma and then she was rushing back to finish an essay.

'But she's nineteen isn't she?' said Ellie, after the two older girls had left. 'Surely she doesn't have to go to school?'

'Sian ees at university,' Camille explained. 'She

took a year out to do ze Olympics but now she ees studying again.'

'Most of the other Senior Elite girls train full time, but Sian reckons it's easier to be disciplined if she's doing stuff outside gym too,' added Kashvi with a shrug. Out of her leotard, she was less of a princess and more of a tomboy. 'Go figure!'

'Wow,' said Ellie, who was already feeling a bit nervous about juggling schoolwork and gym.

'Yup, basically any time Sian's not spinning through the air at impossible speeds she's got her head in a book,' said Nancy. 'She makes the rest of us look totally lazy!'

'What's she studying?' Ellie asked, fascinated by the older girl's focus and commitment.

'Italian and Russian!' said Nancy. 'Which means she must be a super-brain as well as the best gymnast in the country. It's not fair – I figure anyone that good ought to be really stupid, or at least really ugly, or something to balance things out. Some people have all the luck.'

The girls made their way outside but Ellie

remembered that she'd left her guard bag in the changing room. Embroidered with her name, Mum had made it for her when she'd got her first ever pair of hand-guards. She was cross with herself for being so forgetful.

'I'll catch up with you,' she called to the others as she darted back inside. She quickly ran into the changing room and picked up the bag. As she was making her way out, she bumped into someone in the corridor.

'I'm so sorry, I . . .'

She looked up and realised she had run headlong into Sian Edwards herself.

'Oh, don't worry. But . . . hey . . .' Sian stopped and stared curiously at Ellie. 'You're the new girl in Development, right? You look kind of familiar. Have we met somewhere before?'

'I don't think so,' said Ellie, whose mouth had gone totally dry. Sian had a kind of luminous quality – she wasn't beautiful exactly, but somehow it was hard to take your eyes off her.

'Maybe at a competition,' Sian was saying. 'Were

you at the English Champs last year?'

Ellie shook her head, too shy to admit she hadn't competed in any of the national competitions yet.

'You look . . . I dunno . . .' Sian shook her head. 'Never mind, it'll come to me. Must be getting old, eh?'

Ellie wished desperately that she could think of something sensible to say, but the only thing that came out was, 'I love your vault. How do you do it?'

Sian laughed. 'Well, being short helps! But apart from that just lots and lots of practice. You should have seen how many times I wiped out before I managed to nail it. Seriously. I was black and blue for weeks.'

Ellie nodded vigorously, relieved to hear that even Sian Edwards didn't always get things right first time.

'Anyway, I have to go,' said Sian. 'I have an essay to write. But I'll see you around. What's your name by the way?'

'Ellie.' She hesitated then muttered quietly. 'Ellie – um – Trengilly.'

'Trengilly.' Sian turned to look at her again. 'Of course. I should have realised. You're related to Lizzie Trengilly?'

'She's my aunt,' Ellie said, blushing.

'Wow.' Sian paused for a second. 'Yeah, that makes sense. You look like her – not just your face but something in the way you move. You know, she was a Senior here when I started,' said Sian. 'All I ever wanted was to be as good as your aunt. She was the greatest ever.'

'I'd like to fulfil her dream one day,' Ellie blurted out, surprised to hear herself admitting this to a stranger. 'I'd like to go to the Olympics and win the medal she missed out on.'

The words came out in a rush and Ellie looked away, embarrassed. But Sian just smiled. 'That sounds like a very good ambition to have, Ellie Trengilly,' she said. 'We Seniors had better watch out!'

CHAPTER
Eleven

'Your aunt is Lizzie Trengilly!'

'Why didn't you say?'

The girls were making their way back across the park. Scarlett, Camille and Kashvi were quizzing Ellie about her conversation with Sian, which Scarlett had somehow managed to overhear.

'I don't know,' Ellie admitted. 'I guess I thought you all knew.'

'If any of you had bothered to actually read Ellie's name on the noticeboard properly, you would have!' said Nancy. 'It's hardly like she was making a secret of it.'

'Of course, that explains it,' said Scarlett with a toss of her perfect blonde hair.

'Explains what?' said Nancy.

'Well, when I overheard Emma telling Sasha they were giving a scholarship to a girl who'd only just got her Grade Three I couldn't figure it out. But now it all makes sense. She took you because of your name.'

Ellie felt her cheeks blaze red.

'That's not fair!' said Nancy angrily.

'Nancy's right. That's an awful thing to say,' protested Bella.

'But it doesn't make it any less true,' said Scarlett, looking at Ellie with a gleam of triumph in her eye.

Tam came running up to join them. 'What's all this?' He'd been walking back from training with some of the boys' squad, but his teammates had all headed towards the tube station.

'Ellie's only related to Lizzie Trengilly!' said Kashvi.

'Duh – yeah!' said Tam. 'Have you only just figured that out? Everyone in the boys' squad was talking about it today. She's even called Ellie which is short for Elizabeth – am I right?'

79

'Um – yes,' Ellie stammered. 'My dad named me after his sister because apparently I kept doing somersaults in my mum's tummy when she was pregnant.'

'Ah – zat ees so sweet!' said Camille.

'Hmmph!' said Scarlett, less impressed. 'Well, it's very convenient that the little nobody from a gym no one's ever heard of mysteriously gets a place at the Academy and then turns out to have a super-famous relative who just so happens to have been teammates with Emma Bannerdown.'

'Stop right there before you say something you really regret,' said Tam, a flash of anger flickering across his normally twinkly brown eyes.

'Or which I *make* you regret!' muttered Nancy.

Ellie was frozen to the spot, trying desperately to hold back the tears that were pooling in her eyes. She wanted to say something, but all she could think was what if Scarlett was right? She was way behind the others. What if she didn't deserve to be there after all?

'Just wait. Ellie will prove she has as much right

to be here as any of us,' said Tam. 'Probably more, in fact.'

'Oh, and how do you reckon that?' said Scarlett with a sneer.

Tam looked Scarlett up and down then smiled slowly. 'You've been coming to the Academy since you were four years old, right?' He didn't wait for a response before going on. 'And I'm not saying you only got picked for Beginner's squad because your parents paid for the new pit, but it was funny how you got in the exact same year, wasn't it?'

Kashvi and Camille giggled and Nancy hooted with laughter. Even Bella had a twinkle in her eye. Scarlett looked livid.

'Private lessons, top choreographers for your routines, a leotard for every day of the year,' Tam went on. 'No wonder you're ahead.'

He paused for a second before nodding in Ellie's direction. 'Ellie's made it this far without any of that stuff. And if she can get this good in a local gym club, just think how great she'll be after a bit of time at the Academy.'

Scarlett flicked her hair, but her face had gone pale. For a moment she seemed lost for words, then she glared at Ellie and said spitefully, 'Well, there may not be any famous gymnasts in my family, but at least we're not so poor I have to wear second-hand school uniform!' Then she turned on her heel and stormed off.

Nancy looked as if she was ready to run after Scarlett and rugby tackle her to the ground. 'Ooh, she makes me so mad!' she growled. Then she turned to Ellie and linked arms with her. 'But just ignore her. She's only being like that because she's jealous. You get that, right?'

Ellie smiled weakly. She was grateful to Tam and Nancy for standing up for her. She'd been here less than a day and already felt as if she had made great friends. But as they made their way back to Head-Over-Heels House, Scarlett's accusation rang in her head, adding a tiny drop of sourness to her otherwise perfect first day as an Academy girl.

CHAPTER
Twelve

It didn't take long for Ellie to settle in to the hectic rhythm of life at the Academy: early starts four days a week, gym after school every day except Wednesday, a long gym day on Saturday and then Sunday was a rest day.

'If you call doing homework and laundry and having to tidy your bedroom and do a million chores a rest!' moaned Nancy.

All the girls at Head-Over-Heels House were expected to do their bit. Sian Edwards might have won Olympic gold but she still took her turn on the washing-up rota. They might grumble occasionally, but nobody really minded helping out. It made Head-Over-Heels House feel like a home – like they were all part of one big gymnastic family.

Ellie spoke to her real family nearly every day. Lucy had set up Skype at home so Ellie could look straight into the kitchen of Trengilly Cottage where the family would crowd around the computer screen to chat to her.

Lucy wanted to hear all the details of Ellie's life at the Academy – every bruise, every technique, every new move Sian Edwards managed to master.

'Don't you ever get bored of this stuff, Lucy?' Ellie asked one day after a long conversation about Oleg, whose new obsession was to get the girls in Pre-Elite to eat germ-busting foods. Last week it had been spinach and the week before it had been strange-tasting dried fish, which had stunk out the gym for days.

'No way!' said Lucy. 'I need to know it all for when I come to the Academy, you know. I've been working really hard – practising on the beach every day like you used to. Fran says my floor work is looking good – she thinks it's because I do ballet too. I just need to build up my strength cos I'm not as muscly as you are.'

'Just keep working and it'll come,' said Ellie, impressed by the look of fierce determination on Lucy's face.

'What about you?' Lucy asked. 'Are you excited about going for Grade Two? When you pass you'll be eligible to compete at British Champs!'

'*If* I pass,' said Ellie. She didn't want to admit, even to Lucy, that she was terrified about the make-or-break national grade competition that was getting closer day by day. It was a huge step up for her and there was so little time to master the compulsory moves that it sometimes felt like an impossible task.

'Of course you'll pass!' said Lucy. 'You'll probably win the whole competition. And then you'll go to the British and win a gold medal. I know you will!'

Ellie couldn't help feeling pleased that Lucy believed in her, and she desperately hoped she was right. Not about the gold medal – just passing the grade and *getting* to the British would be good enough for her. She knew that she'd improved a lot even in the short time she'd been at the Academy, and Sasha seemed pleased with how she was doing, but she still didn't feel nearly ready for Grades. And she *had* to be ready – because, although nobody had said it exactly, she knew her scholarship depended on her qualifying. And there was no way Mum and Dad could afford for her to stay without it.

She quickly changed the subject. 'Did I tell you Tam and Nancy keep promising to take me sightseeing? Leicester Square and the London Eye and Oxford Street and all those places.'

'Wow!' said Lucy.

'But somehow we're always so busy there never seems to be any spare time,' said Ellie.

'You can't live in London and not see the sights!' said Lucy.

'Tell you what, when you come and visit, we'll all go together.'

'But that's ages away!' moaned Lucy. 'Not till after half term!'

'I know,' sighed Ellie. 'But Emma reckons it's

for the best. No family visits for the first few weeks while you settle in. Apparently, it's to stop you getting homesick.'

'Well, it seems like a silly rule to me!' said Lucy. 'I bet you're having way too much fun to miss home anyway!'

Ellie *was* having an amazing time at the Academy, but she missed her family and the creek more than she admitted to Lucy. Sometimes it felt like a dull ache in her heart that wouldn't quite go away, and at others it would rush suddenly over her like a wave, usually when some sight or smell reminded her of Cornwall. She dreamed of the creek every night and woke each morning longing for the feel of sand between her toes and salt spray against her skin.

Mandy was incredibly sweet. As Head-Over-Heels housemother she was used to helping new gymnasts through homesickness, so she was always the first to spot if Ellie was pining for home. She always seemed to know just how to take Ellie's mind off things, dragging her into the kitchen to help bake a cake or sitting her down for a cup of a tea and a chat.

And there wasn't really much time to feel sad – she was always in the gym! But Scarlett's words kept nagging at her. Ellie was determined to get everything right, to prove she really deserved to be there, but although she *knew* she was getting better, there was something in her gymnastics that was niggling at her too.

At the end of one evening training session, Ellie was practising her new floor routine for Grades. She had no trouble landing the tumble sequences but for some reason her dance elements felt off. She couldn't seem to let her imagination take over like it usually did when she performed. She finished the routine knowing she had nailed the new moves Sasha had added, but still feeling oddly empty and dissatisfied.

Sasha could see something was up, and she kept Ellie back after the session.

'You're doing really well,' she said, looking at Ellie closely. 'Everyone is very impressed with your attitude and your ability to pick things up so quickly.'

Ellie smiled nervously, sure there was a 'but' coming.

'But I feel as if something's holding you back,' Sasha went on. 'You're getting the techniques, your range and conditioning is nearly there and even your beam is improving.'

Ellie waited for another 'but' and there it was . . .

'But I'm worried about you,' Sasha said gently. 'Are you unhappy at the Academy?'

'No,' said Ellie truthfully. 'I – I love it here. I've never been more excited about anything in my life.'

'That's good to know,' said Sasha with a smile. 'We want our gymnasts to be happy. And it's not that you seem sad exactly. More that there's something not quite – right.'

'Oh,' said Ellie, unsure what to say or how to feel.

'Why not go away and think about it,' said Sasha, her tone more serious than usual. 'Usually a gymnast knows this sort of thing in her heart. It just takes a bit of digging to find it.'

'Um – right,' said Ellie.

'Go and search for your missing ingredient!'

smiled Sasha, back to her usual chirpy tone. 'The topping to your muffin, the icing on your bun. And I look forward to seeing you as a perfect Ellie-cake before we know it.'

CHAPTER
Thirteen

'Apparently I'm like a cake without a topping, or I'm missing a flavour or something,' Ellie said when Tam and Nancy asked her about the conversation later that evening. The three of them were sitting around the dining table at Head-Over-Heels House. Most of the other girls had gone to the cinema and Sian and Sophia were away at another training camp. Tam and Ellie had agreed to stay behind to help Nancy with her maths homework.

'What – like rainbow sprinkles or chocolate chips?' said Tam.

'Seriously, bro, do you ever stop thinking about food?' said Nancy.

'Food and gymnastics – what else is there worth thinking about?' grinned Tam.

Nancy shook her head and turned back to Ellie. 'So, what did Sasha say exactly?'

'Oh, I don't know,' sighed Ellie. 'I can't work out what I'm doing differently. I'm putting in more hours than I ever did at home – well, in the gym anyway – I used to practice on the beach a lot.'

'Isn't that really difficult?' said Nancy, who was chewing on the end of a giant sparkly pen. 'I'd have thought sand would be tricky, especially if you want to do a turn or something.'

'There are some things you can't do,' said Ellie. 'But I always loved practising outside. My dad even built me some apparatus.'

'Like what?' asked Tam.

'He made me a vault out of bits of old boats lying around the yard,' she said. 'And a beam too.'

Ellie thought of the boat beam her dad had made her. It had a familiar salty smell, and there was something about the feel of the sea-weathered wooden surface under her feet, which had seemed to magically improve her balance.

'And if it rained?' asked Nancy.

'Then I got wet.' Ellie shrugged. 'It's kind of fun doing gymnastics in the rain. You should try it sometime.'

'No thanks!' said Nancy. 'I fall off the beam often enough as it is – if it was slippery I'd have no chance.'

Nancy had been really down about her gymnastics recently – nothing seemed to be going right for her and it was starting to affect her confidence. Most of the time she just joked about it, but Ellie could see that underneath she was really upset.

'What about the bar?' asked Tam. 'You can't do that on a beach. It'd be too dangerous if you fell wouldn't it?'

'Oh yeah, Dad couldn't figure that out at first either,' said Ellie, smiling as she remembered.

'So what did he do?' asked Nancy, who had totally given up on her fractions now.

93

'He went off into his workshop. He was there for hours, drawing and measuring stuff and the next day at low tide he was out on the pontoon banging and welding. He told me and Lucy we weren't allowed to go down to the beach until the tide came in.'

'And then what?'

'Then we saw what he'd done. He'd made this set of uneven bars - out in the water - so that I could use them when the tide was in.'

Tam was staring at her in disbelief. 'Are you seriously telling me that you worked on uneven bars out at sea?'

'Sort of. I mean, it's more of a tidal estuary, but it's still saltwater, I suppose.'

'It's the not the saltiness that's getting me,' said Tam. 'It's the thought of getting plunged in frozen water each time you dismount.'

'Well, it's not that deep,' said Ellie. 'And the creek water only goes below freezing in December and January. Then I can't practice for too long or I go a bit blue. I did try doing it in a wet suit but it was

94

hard to get the flexibility, you know.'

'Um – no, I don't know!' said Tam.

'Ellie Trengilly, you are totally the maddest gymnast I have ever met,' said Nancy. 'I love gym, but nothing – I mean *nothing* – would make me want to practise in cold water. And what about sharks and killer whales and icebergs!'

'There aren't any of those in the creek!' laughed Ellie. 'It's lovely in summer and you're forgetting I'm used to being in the water. Me and Lucy went swimming in the creek all the time, and when you sail you get used to being dunked every now and then. It's no big deal.'

'Well, I think we've solved the mystery, then,' said Tam.

'What?' said the girls, turning to him at exactly the same time.

'Your missing ingredient. It must be the creek, right?' He didn't wait for an answer, but went straight on. 'It's a no-brainer really. I mean, your eyes light up when you talk about it – it's obvious how much you miss it.'

95

'I don't know,' said Ellie, frowning. 'I suppose it could be.'

'I think Tam's right,' said Nancy. 'Which does happen occasionally!'

'Oi!' said Tam.

Nancy ignored him. 'Yup – I think this crazy beach workout routine of yours must be the missing icing on the Ellie-cake!'

'Well, I'm not sure we can build you a set of bars in the middle of the Thames,' Tam said, 'but we have got the park right on our doorstep. Grass is a bit different to sand, but if being outside is your thing, it might work. At least until you get your creek fix at half term.'

'Do you think –' Ellie hesitated, wondering if Tam might be right. She *had* been missing her beach practice sessions more and more recently, especially as the weather improved and she could imagine what the creek was like in the early spring. 'I mean, would we be allowed?'

'There are always yoga classes going on in the park,' said Tam. 'And there are those crazy bootcamp men shouting at people to do press-ups, so I can't see why we wouldn't be allowed to do a few tumbles round the bandstand.'

'But do you think Emma would mind?' Ellie said. 'We're not allowed to practise in the gym without supervision, so would it be OK to do it outdoors?'

'Sasha told you to go and find a spoonful of sugar, or whatever,' said Nancy. 'So we're just following orders.'

'Hey, there's the boating lake too,' said Tam. 'I think it's mainly shut up in the winter, but when it gets warmer you can hire pedalos and stuff. We'd be happy to push you in any time you want a good soaking!'

'Um – thanks, I think!' said Ellie.

She couldn't help grinning as they helped Nancy finish her fractions. She had no idea if this crazy plan was going to make any difference, but she felt really lucky to have friends who cared enough to help. And it had to be worth a try, didn't it?

CHAPTER
Fourteen

Over the next couple of weeks, Ellie, Nancy and Tam spent most of the little free time they had practising in the park. They found a quietish spot, not far from the café by the boating lake where there was a patch of grass big enough to use as a practice floor. Luckily the weather was mild so the ground wasn't too hard. A soft February sunshine dappled the grass and stopped them from freezing to death, although Nancy swore she was growing icicles on her toes.

Sometimes, Mandy made them up a picnic, or they would treat themselves to cakes and creamy hot chocolates from Mario's café after a session.

Ellie loved it. She could let her mind wander when she practised outside. Without a coach watching, and with the sound of the city in the background and the faint whiff of the river nearby, she felt free. It took away some of the tightness that had crept into her gymnastics and she seemed to nail the moves far more comfortably than in the gym.

'You look like some kind of park fairy,' said Nancy, munching on one of Mario's amazing flapjacks and watching her friend whilst sitting in the splits. 'Seriously, all you need is a pair of wings and you could take off at the end of that tumble sequence.'

Ellie laughed. 'It does sometimes feel like flying, doesn't it. Or swimming. Sometimes I imagine I'm a mermaid, darting and diving underwater, you know?'

'Not me!' said Nancy decidedly. 'All I can think about when I perform is Emma glaring at me if I get it wrong.'

Ellie laughed.

'When I compete, I try to calculate my difficulty values and execution scores as I go along,' said Tam, who was walking up and down the grass on his hands. 'I do a running tally in my head the whole time. Stops me being nervous.'

'I guess we all have our own way,' said Ellie. She knew from what some of the other boys had said that Tam was an incredibly talented gymnast – one of the best in the squad, and he'd already passed his Grade Six, which was the top one for male gymnasts – but she privately thought that his approach would have totally put her off. She tried not to think about her scores at all when she performed. It only made her nervous.

'In competitions I get so nervous I can hardly think at all!' Nancy said, standing up and stretching her leg into an elegant arabesque. With her long legs in a pair of pale pink fluffy sweatpants, Ellie thought she looked like a flamingo. 'My mind goes blank and I have to remind myself to breathe.'

'Breathing is definitely important,' said Tam, springing back up on to his feet and then flipping into a backwards somersault in one smooth movement. 'The judges will totally penalise you if you, like, die in the middle of the routine!'

Ellie giggled and watched as Tam flipped back on to his hands and started spinning his legs round in a helicopter movement as if he was on the pommel horse. He was so strong and he had a quiet confidence, unlike Nancy who was doubting herself more and more.

'I bet Scarlett just thinks about lifting the trophy,' said Nancy, rolling her eyes. 'Eyes on the prize at all times that girl.'

'Whatever works, I guess.' Ellie frowned as she thought of Scarlett, who hadn't been any friendlier to her. In fact, she seemed to get frostier whenever Ellie did something right, and revelled in every stumble or missed landing. 'But the only way I can get past my nerves is to pretend it's not a competition at all. That I'm somewhere else. On the bar I imagine I'm a bird and on the vault I think about being a leaping salmon, thrashing my way upstream.'

'Yup – you're totally weird!' laughed Nancy.

'Personally I feel less like a fish when I'm on the vault and more like a giraffe. Look – I've grown again!' she said, pointing at her long leg stretched out behind her. 'These trousers are too short for me even though Mum only got them at Christmas.'

'Being tall makes you really good at netball,' said Ellie, trying to cheer her friend up. 'Miss Robertson said in PE last week that you could join the school team if you wanted to.'

'That's not going to help me at Grades, though, is it?' said Nancy gloomily. 'Every time I grow another inch it throws all my moves off. And when did you last see a six-foot-tall gymnast – or a girl twin who was taller than her brother?'

'OK, OK, I'm a hobbit! No need to rub it in,' said Tam. 'I could do with a couple more inches on the rings, you know.'

'You're a great gymnast, Nancy,' said Ellie. 'You're so strong, and you've got amazing balance – ten times better than mine. And look at your mum – she was tall and she still made it.' Ellie had discovered that the twins' mum had been an Academy girl herself once upon a time, competing at international level before retiring with an injury in her late teens.

'But Mum grew later,' said Nancy with a shrug. 'She was still quite small till she hit sixteen, so she had a chance to compete at Senior level before she got her growth spurt.' Nancy glared at her long willowy legs as if she blamed them for her extra inches. 'It's all my dad's fault!'

'Was he a gymnast too?' asked Ellie. She didn't know much about the twins' dad, who'd died in a car crash not long after they were born.

Both the twins hooted with laughter. 'No way!' said Tam, pulling himself effortlessly from box splits through an elephant lift to a handstand. 'Dad wasn't into sport at all. He was a six-foot-two accountant by day and a stand-up comedian by night. Mum said he made her laugh so much she agreed to marry him.'

'And he seems to have given me his height genes, but failed to pass on the talent for maths,' said Nancy with a sad smile.

'Well, you did get his talent for being funny,' said Ellie.

103

'I'm not sure how much that will impress the judges at Grades,' said Nancy.

'I don't know. You could include a few jokes in your floor routine,' said Tam, still upside down. 'Throw in the odd one liner while you're on the bar.'

But Nancy didn't even smile at that. Ellie had never seen her friend so sad. Nancy was usually a ball of energy, making a joke of everything, but now she seemed genuinely down.

And Ellie knew she had a point. Nancy *was* struggling. Despite all her worries, Ellie had been making steady progress, but Nancy seemed to be going backwards. Her growth spurt wasn't helping, but it was her lack of confidence that was the main problem. And the closer they got to the competition, the more her nerves seemed to be getting the better of her. Ellie wished she could do something to help – like the twins had helped her.

Suddenly, she remembered the conversation she'd had with her mum last night, about going home to the creek for half term.

'I've got the perfect cure!' she said excitedly.

'For my long legs?' asked Nancy with a grimace. 'It is painful?'

'No, silly! For your competition nerves,' said Ellie.

'Um – a brain transplant?' suggested Tam with a grin. Nancy gave him a shove that made him topple over on to the grass.

'No! You need a change of scene – somewhere you can forget about competitions and cartwheels for a bit! And I know just the place.' Ellie grinned, wondering why she hadn't thought of this before. 'Why don't you both come to the creek with me for a few days?'

'Sounds cool, but – um – won't your parents mind a pair of total strangers landing on them?' said Tam.

'I'll ask them tonight but they're really laid back so I doubt they'll be bothered,' said Ellie. 'Besides, I talk about you both so much you're practically family already!'

'Sea, sand and surfing!' said Nancy, a giant grin spreading over her face. 'It'd definitely make a change from somersaults and splits. Ooh – and you can teach me to row!'

'Exactly!' said Ellie, glad to see her friend smiling again. 'And the creek is magical – a few days there can cure just about anything. You might even shrink in the saltwater.'

'Take me there now!' squealed Nancy.

CHAPTER
Fifteen

Over the next few days, Ellie started to feel that something was different. During one session, Sasha commented on her improved floor routine. 'Much more fluid,' she said, and Ellie felt a warm glow inside. She'd been daydreaming of home as she'd been performing, thinking of the ripple of the waves on the creek when the spring breezes ran over them. You couldn't get much more fluid than that.

'I think it's working,' she whispered to Nancy as she alighted from the beam a couple of days later. 'I think I'm starting to find the topping for my cake!'

'I'm hoping mine's going to turn up in Lost

Property,' said Nancy. 'Otherwise I'm going to be turfed out of Development squad and sent back to a recreational class to learn how to do cartwheels. Do you know, Sasha says I'm not even doing those right any more. I'm properly losing it, Ellie!'

'You just need a holiday,' said Ellie, putting her arm round her friend. 'This time next week we'll be on the beach.'

'Maybe I'll take a metal detector and see if I can find my missing ingredient buried in the sand!' laughed Nancy.

The last few days of term seemed to go by in a blur with preparations for going away, last-minute school assignments and extra training sessions to make up for the ones they were going to miss. And there was huge excitement at the Academy when they turned up on the last day of term to see a notice on the squad board announcing try-outs for the National Team Finals, which were to take place after Easter.

'They need a team of six gymnasts to represent the Academy,' said Bella as everyone crowded around. 'And it says even us Development girls will be considered.'

'Kashvi must be in with a chance,' said Nancy. 'Her floor routine is to die for. I don't have a hope. And I'm not sure the rest of us can go up against Isobel or Mia, or even Bree from Pre-Elite.'

'Speak for yourself,' said Scarlett. 'I'm certainly not going into trials with that defeatist attitude. If you want something, you have to fight for it, Nancy Moffat.'

'She's right,' said Ellie. 'We should all at least try.'

'Well, at least this is one event where your beloved auntie won't help you,' said Scarlett, unzipping her squad tracksuit to reveal yet another new leotard. Nancy reckoned everyone in the gym was in danger of being blinded by Scarlett's sparkle and bling as her leotards got more ornate by the week.

'Um – what's that supposed to mean?' said Nancy.

'Well, I doubt Emma's likely to forget that it was Lizzie Trengilly's fault that Team GB missed out on a gold medal at the Olympics in 2000, is she now?'

said Scarlett gleefully. 'Especially since Emma was in the team.'

'But zey won silver, didn't zey?' said Camille.

'Yes, but they *should* have won the gold!' declared Scarlett. 'And they were going to as well. Right up until the moment Lizzie Trengilly messed up on the beam and blew it all.'

'That's not what happened, is it?' said Bella, looking puzzled.

'Oh, I'm sure the newspapers put some spin on it,' said Scarlett, 'because Lizzie was injured and everyone was feeling sorry for her. But Emma knows the real story.'

Ellie didn't know what to say. She knew that her aunt had landed awkwardly from her beam routine in that competition. That she'd shattered her leg so badly she could never compete again. But she hadn't realised that this is what had cost her team the gold.

'Oh, just ignore her, Ellie,' said Nancy. 'She doesn't know what she's talking about.'

'Don't I?' said Scarlett. 'Why don't you ask your aunt and see? Oh, I forgot – you can't because she's fallen off the face of the planet. You know, she can't think much of your chances as a top gymnast or she might take a little bit more interest in your career, don't you think?'

Ellie felt her face burning up. Scarlett was right. Aunt Lizzie didn't seem the least bit interested in Ellie's gym career.

'Oh, give it a rest, Scarlett,' said Nancy. 'You're forever going on about how Ellie only got into the Academy because of her aunt. Now you're saying she doesn't stand a chance at try-outs because of her. Make up your mind, why don't you! It can't be both ways.'

'Whatever,' said Scarlett. 'There's no way they're going to pick anyone who hasn't passed Grade Two yet anyway. So that counts you both out, doesn't it!' And with that she marched off into the gym.

For the whole of that morning's training session, Ellie couldn't get Scarlett's words out of her head. Everyone else was buzzing about Team Champs but Ellie struggled to feel excited. In fact, the confidence she'd been feeling lately seemed to have deserted her all over again. And she felt wobblier on the beam than ever. She kept thinking about Aunt Lizzie messing up and that seemed to stop her from sticking her own moves – time after time.

Nancy could tell she was still worrying about it when they went to bed that night.

'You can ask your dad about it when we get to Cornwall,' she suggested. 'He must know what happened. Lizzie is his sister after all.'

'He's not exactly a world expert on gymnastics,' said Ellie. 'He calls a Tzukahara vault the Ali Baba, and reckons a round-off flick is called a roundhouse kick!'

Nancy giggled. 'But surely he'll know the truth about this.'

'I guess I can try to talk to him,' Ellie said, still feeling unsure.

'Good,' said Nancy. 'But not too much gym talk. I'm coming to Cornwall to escape from all that, remember. Sunshine and sailing – and lots of rowing lessons too – and not a word about Grades!'

'Well, I can't guarantee the sunshine,' said Ellie. 'But I promise you'll love Cornwall.'

As Ellie drifted into sleep thinking of the creek, she felt calm for the first time that day. She couldn't wait to show Tam and Nancy her home, and to introduce them to Lucy. And she found herself remembering what Fran had said that day on the beach, about keeping Cornwall in her heart. The hectic Academy life wasn't always easy. It would be nice to soak up a bit of creek magic.

CHAPTER
Sixteen

Ellie called home first thing the next morning to remind Mum to pick them up from the station. But when Lucy's face appeared on the Skype screen, Ellie's heart sank. Lucy was covered in spots!

'Oh no! What happened to you?'

'I've got chickenpox,' wailed Lucy. 'All the kids in Beginner's squad had it a couple of weeks ago. The spots just appeared this morning and now I'm covered head to toe.'

'You poor thing!'

'Have you had it, darling?' Mum appeared behind Lucy in the screen and at first Ellie thought she had chickenpox too but then realised she was just covered in more paint splats than usual. 'I can't remember. I think you had mumps once – or was that your sister? And maybe scarlet fever but your dad says that doesn't exist any more – like smallpox – and dodos.'

'I told you, it was me who had scarlet fever,' said Lucy. 'And we both had mumps. I remember because we had to miss the creek regatta one year. But Ellie's never had chickenpox – I'm sure of it.'

'Oh dear!' said Mum. 'What about Tam? And Nancy?'

'Um – I don't know!' said Ellie, panic creeping into her voice.

'Well, I had it when I was small – so I'll be OK because you can't get it twice,' Mum went on. 'But your dad hasn't – and chances are he's already been infected. Of course, we won't know for certain for a fortnight. That's how long it takes for the symptoms to show.'

'Two weeks!' Ellie's head was spinning. 'How . . . how contagious is it?'

'Very, according to the doctor,' said Mum. 'Nastiest strain he's seen for years. Something to do with the warm spring and Spanish chickens – or at least I think that's what he said.'

'Does that mean . . .' Ellie hesitated, hardly daring to say it. 'Can we still come home for half term?'

'Well, I've spoken to one of your coaches at the Academy – a man called Oleg something,' said Mum. 'He was quite hard to understand – kept going off into some foreign language – but he didn't seem to think you and the twins should be exposing yourself to illness. He was most insistent, actually. And then there's the risk of you passing it on to all the other gymnasts, especially just before these Grades you're doing . . .'

'What if I went into quarantine – or isolation or whatever they call it,' said Lucy. 'Just while they were here. So they couldn't catch it.'

'But then there's Dad – and anyone else in the village you may have accidentally infected,' said Mum. 'And apparently it's even more contagious before the spots start.'

116

Ellie stared desperately at the two faces on the computer screen in front of her. Surely there must be some way . . .

'No,' said Lucy, her spotty face looking comically serious. 'I can't be responsible for you getting sick and blowing your big chance, Ellie. We won't let you come home, will we, Mum?'

'I think she's probably right, darling,' said Mum. 'I wish she wasn't but . . .'

'As soon as I'm better we'll come up to London to see you,' Lucy announced. 'I'll even bring you a massive bag of Cornish pasties to make you feel at home.'

Ellie laughed because she thought if she didn't she might cry.

'And it's not too long till Easter holidays,' said Mum. 'The time will fly by with all the work you're doing for your team trials and Grades and British Champs.'

'I probably won't even get to the British,' said Ellie, who was finding it really hard to stay cheerful.

117

'Of course you will,' said Lucy. 'But not if you turn all spotty like me!'

'So that's that,' said Mum. 'You stay safely in London and we'll come to visit you for a weekend as soon as Lucy is better. OK?'

'That would be good, Mum,' said Ellie, blinking back her tears and trying really hard not to show how disappointed she really felt. After all, none of this was Mum's fault – or Lucy's. It was just really, really bad luck. 'You concentrate on getting Lucy better.'

'Oh, I feel so itchy all I want to do is go and jump into the creek,' wailed Lucy. 'Dad reckons the saltwater would help, but Mum's keeping me in quarantine in case I give shingles to any of the old folk in the village. If I don't die of chickenpox I may just die of boredom!'

CHAPTER
Seventeen

When Ellie broke the news to the twins, she could see they were nearly as disappointed as she was, although they tried to make the best of it for her sake.

'I expect you've both had chickenpox already,' she said when she told them.

'Yes,' Tam nodded. 'When we were tiny. Mum says we tied ourselves in so many knots trying to scratch our spots that that's when she realised we were destined to be gymnasts!'

Ellie sighed. 'I'm so sorry. I feel like I'm letting everyone down.'

'Don't be stupid!' said Nancy. 'We'll just have to make our own fun here in London.'

'Yes! We can finally give you the full guided tour,' said Tam. 'The Tower of London, Madame Tussauds – and as many lakes, rivers and ponds as we can Google. So you feel at home, you know!'

Mandy was lovely too, promising to make all Ellie's favourite dishes over half term and offering to take her and the twins to the cinema or a West End show. 'I know it's not quite the same as home comforts,' she said as she sat across from Ellie that evening at dinner. 'But we'll do whatever it takes to make half term lots of fun for you.'

'Thanks,' said Ellie.

'I've already spoken to your mum and made a plan for your family to come and stay in a couple of weekends' time,' she added.

Ellie tried to smile. 'That's great.' She swallowed down her sadness and decided that if she couldn't go home, she would make the most of the extra time to train. Sasha was away, but Emma was around with the Senior Elite girls and had said she would be happy for the younger girls to work on their own as long as one of the coaches or senior gymnasts was in the gym too.

The first couple of days, Tam and Nancy tried to drag her off sight-seeing but Ellie said she wasn't really in the mood.

'I'm going to use this time to get ready for Grades,' she said after the third day, ignoring the anxious look that passed between the twins. 'If I feel more prepared, I'll be more relaxed.'

'But you need to take a break too,' said Nancy. 'All rest and no play, and all that . . .'

Ellie shrugged. 'You know me. I don't see gymnastics as work – it's always been my way of having fun.'

'Well, at least come to the park to practise tomorrow,' said Tam. 'I'm getting withdrawal symptoms from Mario's chocolate muffins – and I can talk Mum into making a picnic.'

Nancy rolled her eyes. 'Food obsessed, that's what you are! But Tam's right – we could work on our floor routines then visit the monkeys in the park zoo!'

'Maybe,' said Ellie. But spring showers hit London, and it was too wet to train in the park the next day, so Ellie hid herself away in the gym again. All the extra hours were definitely helping her technique, but she could feel the old tension creeping back into her work. And, despite what she'd said to Tam and Nancy, she wasn't having as much fun as she normally did.

At the end of the session only Ellie and Sian Edwards were left. As they made their way to the changing room, Ellie rubbed her hip. She'd landed on it over and over again trying to master a pike Yurchenko vault, and now it felt stiff and sore.

'I've seen you here a lot this week, haven't I?' Sian said as she sat down on one of the benches and started to unwrap the supports from round her ankles.

'Yes – I couldn't go home for the holidays,' Ellie explained. 'My sister's ill.'

'And you didn't want to hang out with the others?' Sian asked, studying Ellie. 'Take a break from training for a few days – have a bit of fun.'

'No – I . . . I just love being in the gym,' said Ellie, although she knew she didn't sound very convincing. 'And, anyway, I'm behind all the others. So I have to work extra hard to catch up.'

'I see,' said Sian, carefully folding her ankle tape into her gym bag. 'But, you know, sometimes you need to take a break to stay fresh.'

'I – I suppose.'

'No suppose about it,' said Sian with a smile. 'Everyone knows it takes hard work to make it to the top. But too much work and not enough play can make your work go stale too.'

'Oh . . . OK,' said Ellie, wondering if Sian had seen her messing up on the vault.

'You're a lovely gymnast,' said Sian, zipping her bag closed and standing up. 'And you learn quickly too. So you'll catch up with the others. Just give it time.'

'Th-thank you,' stammered Ellie, who felt suddenly as if her head was spinning. Had Sian Edwards – the Olympic champion – really just told her she was a lovely gymnast?

'But I'd hate to see you burn out,' said Sian, picking up her bag and heading from the door. 'So, promise me you'll take a day or two off?'

Ellie nodded, still reeling from the compliment. 'I will. I promise.'

So Ellie kept away from the gym for the next couple of days and let Tam and Nancy drag her round various museums and galleries. It was still far too wet for gymnastics in the park, but on the second day Mandy treated them all to a boat trip along the Thames. 'Because I know how much you're missing the creek,' she said to Ellie.

It was a kind thought, but it just made Ellie feel more homesick than ever. Staring out of the rain-streaked window of the river cruiser at the brown sludgy river water made her long for the clear waters of home. And nagging at the back of her mind were her worries about that pike Yurchenko – and her beam routine – and finding her secret ingredient. Sian had said she needed to have a break, but switching off wasn't as easy as it sounded.

124

Ellie was glad when term started back up again and she had team try-outs to take her mind off everything else.

'I want you to treat this as if it were an external competition,' Emma told the gymnasts as they lined up on the morning of the trials. 'It may only be myself, Toni, Oleg and Sasha judging – and the boys in the audience, of course.'

Ellie glanced over to the other side of the gym where Tam and the rest of the boys' squad were lounging on benches. The boys' equivalent of National Club Champs wasn't till later in the year so today they were just here to support the girls. Tam had been picked to represent the Academy last year but he'd been careful not to go on about in front of Ellie or Nancy. In fact, Ellie only knew because Nancy had told her. Now Tam gave Ellie a thumbs up and she tried to smile back.

'But I want every one of you to bring your A game,' Emma went on. 'Because every single girl here stands an equal chance of getting a spot. From the very youngest to our most experienced gymnasts.'

Ellie's heart hammered in her chest, a mixture of excitement and nerves. Glancing at her teammates, she could see they all felt the same. Nancy was chewing her nails so hard she looked as if she was going to bite her fingers off, Bella had a glassy, wide-eyed expression, and Scarlett was scowling even more than usual.

'Team Champs is a six-five-four format,' Emma explained. 'Six in a team, five compete on each apparatus and the four top scores on each apparatus count towards the team total. So we need good all-round performers, but we are also looking for *specialists* on each piece – gymnasts who can bring us a really breathtaking score on one or two rotations.'

Ellie listened intently. She was certain her wobbles on the beam had ruled her out as an all-round contender, but Nancy reckoned she was one of the best on the bars – better than some of the girls in the older squads even. Maybe if she could wow on that piece of apparatus in front of the judges today . . .

'But most of all we need gymnasts who can

perform under pressure,' Emma was saying. 'If the team is relying on your score to bring us a medal, it's no good to me how you perform in training. You need to bring it on the day. Because if you don't you won't just let yourself down, you let the whole team down.'

'And she knows how that feels,' Scarlett whispered, glancing at Ellie as she spoke.

Even before Scarlett had spoken, Ellie had been thinking of Aunt Lizzie. That memory must surely be in Emma's mind too – and that couldn't be good for Ellie, could it?

When Emma's pep talk was over, Sasha drew the Development squad girls to one side before they went to their first rotation. 'OK, my lovely ladies,' she said, beaming as if they were about to go to a party, not face their toughest trial yet. 'This is it! Your chance to go up against the big guns, and show them how it's done!'

'I don't think there's any chance of me showing Sian Edwards how to do anything,' said Nancy.

'Except fall flat on your face!' muttered Scarlett.

'Nonsense,' cooed Sasha. 'The bigger they are the harder they fall. And they won't be expecting competition from any of you little chicks so you have the advantage of stealth and surprise.'

'It's not like we're mounting an attack on enemy territory,' pointed out Kashvi, who was looking very glamorous in a sparkly purple and gold competition leotard, her hair pulled up and covered in glittery hairspray. Camille also looked amazing in a white and silver leo, whilst Scarlett was wearing a new custom-made number, which she said her mum had ordered from Hong Kong.

Suddenly, looking down at her Cornish squad leotard, Ellie wondered if she should have made more of an effort. It was pretty old and tatty now – but it was her lucky charm. It had seen her through many local competitions, and she had worn it the day Emma picked her for the Academy.

The only other competition leotard she owned was wrapped up in tissue paper in her wardrobe. It was the leotard her Aunt Lizzie was wearing in the picture at Head-Over-Heels house – the one she had worn at World Championships. She had given it to Ellie years ago, but Ellie had vowed to herself that she wouldn't wear it until she competed for her country on the international podium to make her aunt proud.

Nancy nudged her hard and Ellie realised she'd been daydreaming. Sasha's pep talk was over and the first rotation was about to begin. So this was it. Her first real chance to show she deserved to be at the Academy – if only she could hold her nerve!

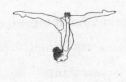

CHAPTER
Eighteen

Ellie was up on vault first. She'd nearly perfected her pike Yurchenko and she was landing it well most of the time – but not *every* time. She knew it was a risk, but it had a high difficulty value – and she knew that was what she needed today.

Oleg was judging vault and he was looking particularly comical in a pair of bright yellow fluffy ear-muffs.

'I heard he's worried about getting ear-worms – or something,' Nancy whispered.

The ear-muffs meant Oleg couldn't hear a word

anyone said and that he shouted very loudly all the time.

'Good luck!' he barked at Ellie, giving her a beaming smile which made his moustache wobble.

Ever since he'd heard about Lucy's illness he'd been extra nice to Ellie, although he did keep offering her some evil-smelling home-made tonic that he swore would keep the chickenpox at bay.

Ellie chalked up her feet then stood at the beginning of the run up, waiting for Oleg to raise an arm as a signal for her to begin. Then she took a deep breath and flung herself into her run up. Things seemed to go in slow motion as she hit the vault and propelled herself into the air, her whole mind and body focused on achieving exactly the right angle of rotation. A few seconds later, she landed. She felt her feet hit the mat, but she'd misjudged it slightly. She wobbled and took a step back.

With a rush of disappointment, Ellie raised her hands. She'd landed that vault perfectly in practice so many times!

'It was only a tiny wobble,' said Nancy as Ellie rejoined the others. Nancy had bombed out completely on her vault – landing with a thud on to her bottom. 'You won't have lost more than half a point – not like my epic fail!'

Nancy's competition nerves seemed to have kicked in hard and she looked as if she was going to be sick. Scarlett, on the other hand, was rising to the occasion. She showed why she was known as Queen of the Beam as she performed a breathtaking routine that couldn't have failed to impress the judges.

'She's better than any of the Pre-Elite or even Junior Elite girls on the beam,' whispered Ellie. 'She's got to be in with a chance of getting a spot on the team.'

'And she knows it!' said Nancy, glancing over at Scarlett who looked like the cat who'd got the cream. 'Which is why you need to wow everyone with that new floor routine of yours and wipe the smile off her face!'

Ellie had always loved the floor, and she'd worked on a complicated new tumble sequence that she hoped would impress Sasha, who was judging. But as she stood waiting for the music to start, she felt a tightness in her chest. As she launched into the opening moves, she was concentrating so hard on her execution that she couldn't switch off.

The routine she gave was technically accurate, but Ellie knew in her heart that she'd lost an element of performance. She'd landed all her tumbles, completed her leap series and her spins without a stumble, but she hadn't felt like a water sprite or a dryad dancing across the floor – she'd just been Ellie Trengilly, trying with every muscle and sinew of her body to get into the squad for Team Champs.

'You were really good,' whispered Nancy when both of them had completed the floor rotation.

'So were you,' said Ellie loyally, although they both knew it was a lie.

'No I wasn't! I stepped out of bounds twice AND I actually forgot my routine at one point!' said Nancy. 'I'm going to pieces, Ellie! I'm totally out of the running now.'

Ellie gave her a hug. She knew that neither of

them were in with a chance yet. To get on the team now they needed to give at least once stand-out performance.

The bar was where Ellie stood her best chance of getting the judges' attention. She'd been working really hard on it since she'd come to the Academy and she was now by far the best bar worker in Development squad.

Sasha reckoned she was ahead of some of the girls in the older squads too. 'Which means if you nail the routine we've been working on, you're still in with a good chance,' she told Ellie as the girls warmed up for their next rotation. 'There are no other bar specialists in the higher squads. Sian's brilliant of course, but it's Sophia's weakest piece. You have a real opportunity here, sausage!'

Ellie wasn't sure if Sasha's words were helpful, or the opposite. And as she chalked up her hands, she could feel the eyes of Toni Nimakov, who was bar judge for trials, watching her keenly, and that seemed to make her more nervous than ever.

But as she was about to mount the bar Tam yelled

from the benches, 'Go on, Ellie! Pretend you're surrounded by freezing-cold water!'

The boys sitting next to him laughed and Ellie could feel some of the other girls giving her funny looks – most of the gymnasts had no idea what Tam was talking about. But Ellie couldn't help smiling. As she launched into the routine, she found herself thinking of the bars in the creek, of the seagulls swooping and diving for fish, of sea breezes curling the ocean into waves that broke and fell. And for the first time all day she let go of the tension she had been carrying in her body and let her longing for the creek carry her through the routine.

When she came off, she realised she had no idea how she'd performed – except that she hadn't messed up or fallen flat on her face, and that she'd landed the complicated double tuck front to finish. Suddenly she wondered if she'd let her concentration slip and blown it, but Tam's beaming face in the crowd told her she'd done well.

'That was amazing!' said Nancy as Ellie returned

to her side. 'Best I've ever seen you do it. That straddle catch was epic!'

'Toni actually stopped writing and stared at you the whole way through,' said Bella.

'It wasn't that spectacular,' said Scarlett.

'Yes it was!' said Kashvi. 'I reckon that's the highest score any of us will have got so far. Ellie could be in with a real chance now.'

'I doubt it.' Ellie shook her head. 'Anyway, I've still got beam to go.'

'Best hope messing up on the beam doesn't run in the family, then,' said Scarlett.

Ellie felt suddenly wobbly again. She'd forgotten about Lizzie for a while, but Scarlett's words had thrown her once more. It wasn't just that beam was always her weakest piece, but also that she suddenly felt really sad. All the years that Lizzie had put in to her training, only for it all to end in heartbreak. For the first time, Ellie thought perhaps she understood why Lizzie had turned her back on gymnastics.

As Ellie approached the beam, she could see Emma looking at her. Was she thinking about Lizzie too? Ellie shook herself – she just needed to forget about all that and focus on doing the best beam routine of her life.

Her mount was faultless and her leap series went without a wobble, and Ellie started to relax and believe she might actually be able to do it. But the acro section – when she had to perform ariels and somersaults on the narrow strip of beam – was always the bit she found hardest, and although she tried to think of her boat beam, she couldn't seem to get the image of Aunt Lizzie out of her head. She landed her flick tuck unevenly and nearly lost it. For a second she thought she was going to fall, but then she regained her control. Now all she had to do was nail her dismount.

She glanced at Emma, and for a second she saw Lizzie, flying through the air and landing to shatter her leg. She hesitated – for one endless moment she thought she might not be able to do it. But she knew she had to finish. So she took a deep breath, pushed all thoughts of Lizzie out of her mind and launched herself off the beam. She was in the air for

137

a second and then . . . she'd landed it. Tight!

It was all over. Ellie had completed all four rotations and there was nothing more she could do. She could definitely have done better on floor, her vault landing had been a mess and she'd hesitated on the beam. Was it too much to hope that maybe, just maybe, she'd made up for it with her bar?

CHAPTER
Nineteen

There was nothing left to do but wait as the judges collated their scores. Ellie had been too focused on her own performance to be aware of how anyone apart from she and Nancy had done. Tam was busy filling her in.

'Sian was top by a mile,' he said. 'And Sophia was great too. Stand out individual performances were Scarlett on the beam, much as I hate to admit it . . .'

'And Mia and Bree were beautiful on floor,' Nancy added.

'You totally nailed your bar,' said Tam. 'And

Issy Mallin was supreme on vault.'

'Well, one thing's for sure,' said Nancy, 'I'm not expecting my name to be called out when they announce the team. I wobbled on the beam, lost it on the floor and crashed and burned on the vault.'

'Your bar was good,' said Ellie.

'But I did it so much better in practice yesterday,' said Nancy. 'I just seem to fall apart in competitions these days. Mum keeps saying I'll grow out of it, only I seem to be growing plenty and there's no sign of the nerves getting any better!'

'I don't expect any of us in Development squad will be picked,' said Ellie, trying to reassure Nancy who really hadn't had her best day.

'I've got my money on Ellie,' said Tam.

'He's right,' said Nancy. 'That bar routine was to die for. I can't wait to see Scarlett's face when they call your name out.'

It felt like the judges were debating forever. Ellie noticed that Sian was looking as nervous as anyone else. Surely she knew her place on the team was safe? But maybe that was the mark of a good gymnast –

never taking anything for granted. And Sian wasn't too nervous to come over to the younger girls and compliment them on their performances.

'You were looking great, all of you,' she said with a warm smile. 'You're certainly giving the Senior Elite squad a run for our money. We need to watch out, don't we, Sophia?'

Sophia grinned. 'None of us is safe with you guys snapping at our heels. I really hope at least one of you makes the squad – you deserve it!'

At last, Emma called all the girls over to the floor, where they sat in a nervous huddle. Ellie squeezed herself between Nancy and Kashvi, near Bella and Camille who were clasping each other's hands tightly. Scarlett sat apart, a confident smile playing about her lips.

'Congratulations, all of you,' said Emma. 'I think the standard was higher than we've ever seen.'

From over on the benches the boys cheered and whooped their agreement. Tam, sitting next to Matt Simmons, was cheering louder than anyone else.

'Picking a team is about trying to balance the

different strengths we have in all our squads,' Emma went on. 'It's about the best combination, not necessarily the top six scorers.'

'Oh, I wish she'd just get it over with,' groaned Nancy quietly. 'The suspense is killing me.'

'So, without further ado: Captain, Sian Edwards.'

Sian stood up and everyone clapped and some of the boys wolf-whistled. The older girl looked as thrilled as if she'd just won her first gold medal.

'Team Second, Sophia Mitford.'

Sophia jumped up with a little squeak and hugged Sian.

Matt Simmons shouted, 'Go, Soph!'

Then Emma read out the names of Isobel Mallin, Bree Summers, Mia Rudolph . . .

'And, finally, I am delighted to announce that our last spot on the team goes to one of our youngest squad members,' said Emma. 'She particularly impressed us on her specialist apparatus.'

Nancy squeezed Ellie's hand and whispered, 'It's you, Kashvi or Scarlett. It has to be.'

'Several members of Development squad

performed strongly, but ultimately this gymnast stood out. So, congratulations to . . .' There was a long pause that seemed to last forever before Emma said, 'Scarlett Atkins.'

Ellie couldn't help the twinge of disappointment. But then she reminded heself – Scarlett hadn't just passed National Grade Two; she'd come third in the whole country. She was supreme on the beam. How had Ellie ever imagined she stood a chance against all that?

Remembering what Emma had said on the first day, Ellie congratulated Scarlett warmly as they made their way out to the changing room. 'You were brilliant today,' she said.

'I was rather, wasn't I!' said Scarlett smugly. 'But you never seriously believed you might get into the team, did you?'

'Um, I . . .'

'I mean, there was no way the Academy was ever going to risk its reputation on a girl who only got a place because of her name,' Scarlett went on. 'Especially when it's the name of the gymnast who blew it all for her team in the Olympics.'

'Seriously,' said Nancy. 'Will you make up your mind? Either being Lizzie Trengilly's niece is a good thing, or it's not.'

'It doesn't matter,' Ellie sighed, wondering once again what exactly she'd done to make Scarlett hate her quite so much. 'Like I said, well done.'

The girls changed and started to make their way home. 'I bet you can't wait to see your family this weekend,' Nancy was saying. 'I just wish me and Tam didn't have to go to Gran's birthday party. I'm dying to meet them.'

As they walked past the coaches' office, Emma appeared and called Ellie back.

'Go on. I'll catch you up,' said Ellie to the others, worried about what Emma might be going to say.

'Better be quick cos it's hot dogs for tea tonight!' said Nancy. 'If you're late, Tam will have eaten them all!'

'How did you feel it went today, Ellie?' Emma asked after the other girls had gone.

Ellie looked down at her feet. 'I tried my best, but . . . well, I guess it wasn't good enough.'

'Well, you're the newest kid in the Academy,' said Emma. 'It was always going to be a tall order going up against girls with the experience of Scarlett.'

'But you said that no one should write themselves off,' said Ellie. 'That it could be a day for giant-slaying.'

Emma smiled, an unreadable expression crossing her face as it often did when she looked at Ellie. 'You know, Toni told me that your bar routine was – let me see if I can recall his exact words. I think they were "like a rainbow". I'm not totally sure what that means, but I do know that he wanted us to consider you for the team.'

'Oh.' Ellie looked up.

'Sasha did too.'

'But *you* didn't think I was good enough.'

'Not yet, no,' said Emma.

Emma spoke bluntly and Ellie couldn't help feeling pained by her words. 'Because I messed up

145

on vault?' she asked, feeling herself flush. 'And hesitated on the beam?'

Emma shook her head. 'Technically, you've made a lot of progress, although you're not completely consistent yet.' She paused. 'But today you seemed – I don't know – disconnected. Your work lacked . . . feeling.'

'Oh,' said Ellie, the words hitting home because she knew, deep down, that they were true.

'When I first saw you, your work was scrappy but it had heart, and passion. That's what Fran told me about you too. You seemed to have lost some of that today.'

Ellie could feel tears springing into her eyes and she blinked hard to keep them back. 'Do you think –' She hesitated, scared of what the answer might be. 'Can I get it back?

Emma narrowed her eyes and tipped her head to one side. 'The thing about this sport is that there's no way of knowing how a gymnast will develop. Some of the brightest young talents burn out early, whilst slow starters show sudden late spurts of brilliance.

There is no magic formula, no crystal ball. All I can say is that you need to keep working on it.'

Ellie thought of all the extra hours she'd put in over half term, her training sessions in the park. What more could she do?

'I'm really trying,' she said, knowing she sounded a bit desperate.

'I know – I've seen you – but I'm still not sure you're bringing everything you can to the gym,' said Emma. 'There's more to being a great gymnast than just developing technique.'

Ellie looked down at her feet, remembering Fran saying something similar that day on the beach. That seemed like a lifetime ago now.

'Anyway, you have another chance to prove yourself at Grades,' Emma went on, matter-of-factly. 'Show me you can put all of yourself into your gymnastics – body, heart and soul.'

Ellie left the gym with a mixture of emotions. She was thrilled that Toni had praised her again, but Emma's comments left her feeling deflated and uncertain.

147

Nancy and Tam were still waiting for Ellie by the park gates.

'Bad luck,' Tam said. 'I thought you were both brilliant.'

'Well, I still think Ellie should have been given a place. Her bar was mind-blowing. Did you see her pirouette?' said Nancy.

'Yeah – I figured you might have had it for a moment there,' said Tam, looking at Ellie who just shrugged. 'I guess you never know what the judges are looking for. Anyway, you two have got Grades coming up. That's what you really need to focus on right now. I mean, Team Champs are fun – but in the end it's all about getting to the British, right?' Tam put an arm round each girl – which was hard since Nancy towered over him.

Ellie let herself be squeezed into the hug and tried to smile. Tam was right – she needed to keep focused on Grades and not let herself get distracted. Emma had made it pretty clear she couldn't afford to mess up again. This time she *had* to prove to Emma that the gamble she'd taken on her had been worth it.

CHAPTER
Twenty

Ellie's disappointment after team trials was washed away by the arrival on Saturday of her mum and Lucy. It wasn't quite as good as going home to the creek, but it was a close second. Lucy had brought a 'parcel of Cornwall' with her that included clotted cream, scones, Cornish pasties and even a jam jar full of sand from Trengilly beach.

'I was going to bring you a bottle of creek water, but Mum was worried you'd drink it and get sick!' she giggled.

The only sad thing was that Dad wasn't with them. Ellie had been looking forward to seeing him too – and she'd wanted to ask him face to face about her Aunt Lizzie and the disaster at the Olympics.

'Dad has the dreaded pox,' explained Lucy. 'And he's a terrible patient, moaning and groaning all the time. We can't get him to stop scratching either.'

Ellie laughed, although she couldn't help feeling sorry for her active dad being stuck in bed.

'He reckons chickenpox is much worse when you're a grown-up,' said Lucy, rolling her eyes. 'But I had way more spots than him so I think he's just being a big baby.'

Ellie smiled at Lucy, thinking how much she had missed her. It was a shame about Dad, but she was determined to make the most of her weekend. It was Lucy's first time in London so she was entranced by absolutely everything – from the black cabs, to the double-decker buses – even the pigeons in Trafalgar Square. And she *loved* Head-Over-Heels House. The twins were away at their grandparents for the weekend so Lucy got to share a room with Ellie while Tam had agreed to let Mum sleep in his room. Scarlett wasn't around either because her parents were in town – which Ellie was secretly relieved about.

Lucy got so excited about meeting the other gymnasts in Head-Over-Heels House that Bella said she felt like a celebrity.

'I've heard so much about you it almost feels like you are!' said Lucy, flushing pink with excitement.

'Hardly!' Bella giggled. 'The only star here is Sian Edwards, but she's training. Hey – why don't you take Lucy and your mum to the Academy?' she suggested to Ellie. 'They could see where you spend most of your time – and maybe get Sian's autograph too.'

Ellie glanced at her sister, who looked as if she might explode with excitement at the suggestion.

'You do realise it's only a regular gym, right? The floor isn't paved with gold and the beam isn't encrusted with diamonds.'

'I know,' gulped Lucy. 'But just think of all the amazing gymnasts who've trained there!'

'Are you sure you wouldn't rather do more touristy stuff?' said Ellie.

'Nope!' said Lucy flatly. 'There is nowhere –

151

nowhere – I'd rather see than your Academy.'

Mum was desperate to visit a couple of new art exhibitions that were showing in London so she whizzed off to the Tate and the National Gallery whilst Ellie took Lucy to the Academy. Lucy was wide-eyed with excitement as they walked in, exclaiming over everything from the cramped changing rooms to the cabinet displaying all the trophies won by Academy gymnasts over the years.

Then they stood by the viewing window, watching the Senior Elite girls train. For the first time since she'd arrived Lucy fell silent.

'Wow!' she breathed as the session came to an end. 'Can you do all that stuff, Ellie?'

Ellie laughed. 'No way!'

'But you might be able to one day.'

Ellie shrugged. 'I don't know – I'd love to think so.'

'Me too,' confessed Lucy. Then she turned to Ellie, her eyes shining. 'Did I tell you I've been promoted to the Junior Competition squad? And Fran says if I work really hard I might even be able to enter for Compulsory Grade Four next year.'

'That's amazing, Lucy!'

'I know. And coming here – seeing the Academy – it's made me want it even more than ever!'

'Well, I can't think of anything better than us both being Academy girls,' grinned Ellie.

'You must be Ellie's little sister!' said a voice behind them.

They spun round to see Sian and Sophia, who had come out of the changing rooms.

'I'd recognise that Cornish accent anywhere,' said Sophia with a smile.

'And you have the same eyes too!' Sian said, stepping forward and offering Lucy her hand. 'I'm Sian, by the way.'

'Yes – I – I – know,' stumbled Lucy, who had flushed bright pink. 'You were . . . I mean, I love . . . that is . . . um . . .'

'This is Lucy,' said Ellie, coming to her rescue.

When Lucy finally recovered enough to speak, Sian signed dozens of autographs for her to take back to her squad mates in Cornwall and then patiently

answered about a million questions on everything from leotards to the Olympics. By the time they left the Academy, Lucy was practically walking on air.

'What do you want to do now?' asked Ellie.

'I don't think anything could ever top that!' sighed Lucy.

CHAPTER
Twenty-one

Over the next day and a half, Ellie showed her mum and Lucy all her favourite haunts – the park, the boating lake, Mario's café, the best walks along the river, where she went to school. Lucy wanted to know every detail of her life in London.

'I just wish I'd got to meet Tam and Nancy,' said Lucy as they sat in Mario's café on Sunday afternoon. Mum was off looking at the paintings in the Park Gallery and the girls were enjoying the very last of their time together before Mum and Lucy headed back home.

'I know – because you'll completely love them!'

155

said Ellie. 'Tam is really funny, and so is Nancy, although half the time she doesn't even realise it. And they're both amazing gymnasts – although Nancy doesn't seem to know that either.'

'Doesn't she?'

'She failed her Grade last year and it really knocked her confidence,' said Ellie, who couldn't help wondering how she'd feel if she missed out at Grades in a couple of weeks' time.

'I kind of wish I'd met Scarlett too,' said Lucy. 'Although I don't much like the sound of her.'

'Oh, she's – I don't know.' Ellie sighed. 'She's always saying I don't deserve to be at the Academy – like I only got in because of Aunt Lizzie.'

'But that's not true!' protested Lucy.

'Maybe. But I guess I just have to prove it,' said Ellie with a shrug.

Mario, the café owner, came over with a plate piled high with buns. 'Ah, this must be the sister of my gymnast friend!' he said when he saw Lucy. 'The hair it is different, but the eyes – they are family eyes, I think. Are you a gymnast too, little one?'

'Yes, and I'm going to come to the Academy one day,' said Lucy, grinning.

'Then one day you will be a regular at Mario's café too. My buns make your sister and her friends somersault higher, you know.'

'It's true,' smiled Ellie. 'They're magic buns. Nancy reckons if we eat enough we'll be Olympic Champions!'

'Yes, yes – and then I will call this new cake "Olympico Muffin" and tell all the world about the famous gymnasts who used to come to my café!' said Mario, waving his arms enthusiastically.

'I don't know about the Olympics – I've got to pass Grade Two first,' laughed Ellie.

'Are you excited?' Lucy asked as they tucked in. 'About Grades.'

Ellie hesitated. 'I'm really nervous,' she admitted. 'I *have* to pass Grade Two, because –' She stopped and looked at Lucy, who was eyeing her anxiously. 'Because if I don't I'm not sure how I can stay at the Academy.'

'What do you mean?'

Ellie felt nervous about sharing her deepest fear, even with Lucy. But she had to tell someone or she would burst . . .

'My scholarship. There's no way they'll renew it if I fail, and Mum and Dad can't afford for me to be here without it.'

Lucy's face fell. 'But – I mean, we'd think of something – wouldn't we? We'd have to.'

Ellie thought about Lucy's ambitions to come the Academy. If Ellie messed up, that would never happen.

'No,' said Ellie. 'It's simple. I have to pass Grade Two – or come home.'

'Sorry I'm late!' Mum came bounding towards them, looking crazy as usual in a purple-and-orange smock that clashed with her pillar-box-red hair. 'Lost track of time . . . We don't want to miss the train, though, so we'd better get a move on, girls.'

'Oh.' Ellie felt a sinking feeling in her stomach as she realised the visit was nearly over. It felt as if they'd only just arrived.

'Don't worry,' whispered Lucy, linking arms with

her as they made their way back across the park to Head-Over-Heels House. 'You'll be fine! I know you will.'

Ellie hugged her sister tightly, wondering how she'd ever bear to say goodbye to her. But in the end, waving Mum and Lucy off wasn't as awful as she'd feared. The fact that Mum couldn't find the tickets and they nearly missed the train kind of helped – because it was all too much of a rush for tears. And, even as she waved off the train, Ellie realised that she felt lighter – happier than she had for ages. The visit had definitely done her good.

Lying in bed that night, she could smell the seasalt from the shells that Lucy had arranged along the windowsill and she knew if she held one to her ear she would hear the soft lapping of waves. It made her feel as if Cornwall wasn't so very far away after all.

CHAPTER
Twenty-two

For the next two weeks, Ellie worked harder than she'd ever worked in her life. There were tests and assignments for school, on top of extra training in the run-up to Grades. Some of the other girls complained, but Ellie found she was enjoying the intensity of the new schedule. Since Mum and Lucy's visit she'd felt different in the gym - freer somehow.

Now she found as she worked on her floor routine her mind was full of the stars shining over the creek and as she turned on the bar she thought of waves curling over the sand banks. She knew her vault still wasn't quite right and there were elements of her beam routine she definitely needed to work on, but still everything felt better and she began to feel more confident about the challenge coming up.

But for Nancy the increased workload was having the opposite effect. The closer they got to Grades, the more tense she became. She started making silly mistakes, and seemed to be having real trouble concentrating.

'It's just nerves,' said Tam as he and the girls were making their way back across the park after a particularly gruelling training session. Nancy had fallen off the beam several times, forgotten her floor routine and done a terrible belly flop off the bar. 'Remember what you were like last time you took Grade Two? You started sleepwalking and everything.'

'Mum found me trying to do a flick tuck on my bed,' Nancy explained. 'I was fast asleep and I stuck it just fine. Maybe I need to be put to sleep just before Grades!'

'You also tried to vault over my bed and nearly squashed me to death in my sleep,' said Tam. 'Seriously, your nerves are a danger to all of us!'

'Mum keeps trying to talk to me about all this competition psychology stuff,' said Nancy. 'She even bought me a load of aromatherapy candles, but nothing seems to be working.'

Tam and Ellie helped Nancy as much as they could, finding time for extra park sessions to build up her confidence. Nancy complained that all this slave-driving was going to kill her, but in fact a couple of days before grades it was Ellie who was feeling under the weather.

She had always been very healthy and hardly ever missed any days of school for sickness, so she was surprised to find herself headachey and slightly dizzy during a training session the day before the competition.

'Are you OK, pumpkin?' Sasha enquired. 'You look a bit peaky.'

'I – I'm fine,' said Ellie. But she didn't feel fine. On the beam she felt weirdly wobbly, and not in the usual way. It was as if she was swimming underwater and the current was pulling her off in all different directions. And as the session went on her limbs felt heavier and achier by the minute. Maybe she'd been training too hard and just needed to take a rest. Sasha had said that they needed to ease up a little before the competition, to give their muscles time to regenerate, but Ellie had been pushing herself to the limit every day.

That night, Lucy Skyped to wish her luck. It was a couple of days since she'd been in touch. 'Everyone sends their love. Dad's down at the boatyard, but he asked me to blow a big kiss your way.'

'Is he better now?' asked Ellie.

'Oh, yes. And Mum's feeling a bit better today too,' Lucy told her.

'What?' said Ellie. 'I didn't know she'd been ill.'

'Oh, she refused to admit it. You know how she is. She only had a few spots so she reckoned she just had a rash.'

'But she's – I mean it can't be chickenpox cos she's had them before,' said Ellie, a pulse

163

of anxiety fluttering in her stomach even as she said it. 'You can't get them twice, right?'

'That's what we all reckoned too, but apparently some people do,' shrugged Lucy. 'It's pretty rare, but it does happen. And with Mum it was so mild that none of us really noticed. She was just a bit dizzy, but Mum's sort of always like that anyway so none of us thought anything of it.'

'Dizzy?' said Ellie, suddenly remembering how she'd felt on the beam earlier.

'Oh yes, I was wobbly too. Just before the spots came out. That's when you're most contagious of course – must have been about a fortnight ago for Mum . . .' Lucy stopped and a look of horror crossed her face. 'That was around the time we came to see you. You don't think . . .'

'No,' said Ellie, pushing away the awful fears that were crowding in her mind. 'I feel fine.'

'I never thought of it till now. Because we didn't even realise Mum had chickenpox for ages. But now I think about it . . . I mean, I hope we haven't given it to any of your friends.'

'All the other girls here have had it,' said Ellie. 'They were all swapping chickenpox stories when you were ill. And you said getting it twice is really unusual – right?'

'Yes. The doctor says Mum's a bit of a one-off. But what about you?' said Lucy. 'If you're going to get it, it'll be any day now.'

'Well, I feel fine,' Ellie lied. 'Never better. I'll be fit as a fiddle for Grades tomorrow!'

Ellie didn't tell Nancy or Mandy or anyone about her conversation with Lucy. Nor did she tell anyone that she was feeling hot and headachey that night when she went to bed earlier than usual. She just said she wanted to get plenty of rest before Grades, like Sasha had instructed.

That night, she dreamed of being back at the creek, rowing on *Jorian*, crabbing off the pontoon, somersaulting on the beach. Except that everything looked different. She couldn't figure out what it was until suddenly she noticed: everything was covered in spots – the crabs, the boat, the houses, even the sky – big red polka dots that seemed to dance before her eyes and made her feel dizzier than ever.

CHAPTER
Twenty-three

Ellie woke up feeling even worse. Her limbs were achy, her head was stuffy . . . and her skin felt oddly itchy.

Her worse nightmares were confirmed when Nancy stared at her sleepily across the room then sat bolt upright in her fluffy kitten onesie and gasped, 'Ellie, what's happened? You're covered in spots!'

'What? No – I can't be. I . . .' Ellie jumped out of bed and rushed to the mirror. Sure enough, there were bright red pustules all over her face. When she pulled up her top, she saw they were peppered over her tummy and arms and legs too.

'No!' she wailed. 'It's Grades today. What am I going to do?'

There was nothing Ellie could do, except stay in bed, drink lots of water, cover herself in calamine lotion to reduce the itching – and watch as the other girls got ready to head off to the competition. She had tried in vain to persuade Mandy she should be allowed to go. 'Now the spots are out I'm hardy contagious at all,' Ellie said. 'Apparently the only way I can pass it on is if somebody actually licks my skin.'

Mandy laughed, but then her face was serious. 'I know how much this means to you, but there's no way the competition organisers would allow you to take part. You're in no condition to compete.'

'I'm fine, I –'.

Mandy raised an eyebrow. 'I doubt you'd be able to stop itching long enough to complete a bar routine. And as for the beam – when you're suffering from dizziness, it simply wouldn't be safe.'

'But if I don't pass . . .' Ellie couldn't bear to finish her sentence.

'I spoke to Emma and she said you shouldn't even think about that right now,' said Mandy. 'Just concentrate on getting better. And then, when you're over the worst, Emma thinks you should go home for a few days. To recuperate and get your strength back.'

'But I –'

'No buts. It's an order from the top. Rest and recuperation are what you need. And believe me when I say that Oleg is not going to let you back into the gym until every single trace of the pox has gone.' Mandy smiled and Ellie couldn't help but grin at the thought of Oleg's reaction. 'He nearly hit the roof when he found out you'd come down with it. I think he considers you as some kind of plague victim.'

'He sent me some blueberries and spinach,' said Ellie. 'Bree dropped them by after training – on her way to school. And more of his home-made Romanian health tonic, which smells so disgusting I think it would kill me sooner than cure me!'

Ellie lay on one of the sofas in the shared lounge,

trying not to feel sorry for herself. She concentrated instead on sending good vibes to her teammates – especially Nancy who had left for Guildford in a very gloomy state, certain that she was going to fail on every piece of apparatus.

The day seemed to drag on forever, but eventually Ellie heard the front door clatter and noisy voices filling the hallway. Bella was the first to appear. She peeked her head around the door and whispered, 'Are you OK? Can we come in?'

'How did it go?' Ellie sat bolt upright, forgetting all about her itchy spots. 'Tell me everything.'

'Well, I came fourth, which means I'll go to the British as one of the top ranked gymnasts!' said Scarlett, strutting in and sitting triumphantly in the most comfortable armchair without even bothering to ask how Ellie was doing.

'And we all passed the grades we went in for!' beamed Bella, then her face creased into a frown. 'Well, everyone except . . .'

But Bella didn't need to finish because Nancy had appeared in the doorway and the look on her face told Ellie everything.

'I missed it by two marks,' she said quietly. 'Just two! But it might as well have been two hundred.' She flopped down on to the fluffy rug by the TV. 'You only get three chances and I've blown them all. I'm going to get kicked out of the Academy for sure.'

'Did Emma say that?' asked Ellie, feeling even more sorry for Nancy than she did for herself.

'Not in so many words,' said Scarlett. 'She said Nancy needed to "take a break" but we all know what that means.'

'Not necessarily,' said Bella, although she was looking anxious too.

'She said I should go away with you and we'd talk about it when I got back,' said Nancy. 'But I'm sure that means I'm out.'

'Oh, but that's brilliant!' said Ellie. 'Oh – I mean, not brilliant that you think you're going to get kicked out – which of course you won't – but that you're coming to Cornwall! And no one can be sad by the seaside, remember – that's what my dad always says.'

171

'Well, I'm looking forward to testing the theory,' said a voice from the doorway.

'Tam, you're back!' Nancy shrieked. Then her face fell. 'Did you hear I failed again?'

'Mum told me.' Tam came and sat next to Nancy and wrapped his arm round her. He didn't say anything – it was as if he didn't need to – and for once Nancy didn't shove him away.

'So are you coming to the seaside too?' she said.

'If Ellie can put up with the two of us,' said Tam. 'I just checked with my coach, Robin. There are no competitions coming up for the boys till June and school breaks up on Wednesday so I can take a whole fortnight off, just as long as I promise to do conditioning exercises every day.'

'Oh, it's going to be brilliant!' said Ellie. Right then she could almost forget about her disappointment, and the horrible itching, and her sadness for Nancy. And even her own fears about her future at the Academy. Because she was going home – and taking her two best friends with her.

CHAPTER
Twenty-four

A few days later, when Ellie felt well enough to travel, she and the twins packed their bags for the trip south. As Mandy bundled them on to the train at Paddington, she told the twins not to drive Ellie's family mad.

'You're going to be lonely without us – admit it!' said Tam.

'I'll enjoy the peace and quiet,' said Mandy, pulling the twins into a massive hug to show she'd miss them really.

'Don't worry – it's only two weeks. We'll be back under your feet again before you know it!'

said Nancy, wiggling free.

'It'll probably take me that long to tidy up your room, young lady!' laughed Mandy. 'Not your side, Ellie. I know which of you it is who makes all the mess!' she added with a wink.

It was strange being back on the same train again, only this time heading in the opposite direction. And as the tower blocks outside gave way to rows of terraces and then green fields, Ellie was surprised to realise she was going to miss London. She hadn't known until that moment how much she'd come to love the city.

Tam pulled out a pack of cards. 'Do you know how to play Cheat?' he asked Ellie.

She shook her head.

'Basically, you have to be good at telling lies,' Tam explained, dealing out the cards.

'And I'm brilliant at it!' said Nancy happily. She seemed much more cheerful since leaving London. 'I can tell the biggest whoppers and keep a totally straight face. Even Tam can't tell if I'm telling the truth.'

'And twins are supposed to be able to read each other's minds, or whatever,' said Tam.

'Yeah – well, I'm glad I can't read yours,' said Nancy. 'It's probably full of football and cars and smelly socks and stuff!'

Tam threw a card at her. 'Well, if you could, you'd see me thinking that I wish you'd shut up so I can show Ellie how to play.'

The game was hilarious and they played for hours as the train wound its way through the English countryside. Nancy turned out to be amazing at the game – just as she'd predicted – and incredibly competitive. After winning for the fifth time in a row she jumped up and declared, 'If this was an Olympic sport, I'd totally be a gold medallist by now!'

Ellie looked at her friend's shining face – so different to the desolate expression she'd worn almost permanently since Grades. It reminded her of the photos she'd seen of Nancy as a little girl, holding trophies she'd won at gymnastic competitions, beaming ecstatically. There was a time when gymnastics had made her this happy too, Ellie thought.

As they played, they munched on the ginormous packed lunch Mandy had made for them, and even though there was enough food to feed a small army, they'd polished it off by half past eleven.

'I'm having another growth spurt,' said Nancy as she beat Tam to the last sausage roll. 'What's your excuse for being a total pig, *little* bro!' She grinned as she said the word 'little'. 'You do realise I'm two inches taller than you now? Looks like I got all the height genes in the family.'

'And I got the good looks and the brains!' Tam retorted quickly.

Once they got past Exeter, Ellie and the twins stared out of the the window, desperate to catch the first glimpse of the sea.

'First one to see the sea gets to make a wish,' Nancy said.

'And eat the last doughnut,' Tam added.

Ellie thought she could guess what Nancy's wish would be. As for herself, she just wished she knew what was going to happen to them when they got back to the Academy.

'There it is!' yelled Tam, jumping up and nearly hitting his head on the luggage rack. 'The sea – it's over there!'

And, sure enough, there it was, a smudge of blue on the horizon. Ellie felt her heart lift.

'I'm wishing for ice cream – every day. And cream teas and Cornish pasties – and sunshine, lots and lots and lots of it!' said Tam.

Ellie smiled and silently made her own wish – she wished that Emma would give her and Nancy another chance.

And then, before she knew it, they were at Truro and she was tumbling out of the carriage and making her way down the platform. Suddenly she heard a high-pitched shriek and Lucy crashed into her.

'You're back!' Lucy yelped, and Ellie felt the breath being squeezed out of her.

'Whoa, when did you get so strong, Lucy!' she grinned as Lucy looked up, her cheeks bright with excitement.

'It must be all the extra conditioning I've been doing!' Lucy said happily, before turning shyly to the twins. 'You must be Nancy,' she said, blushing. 'And Tam. I – I'm Lucy.'

'Of course you are,' said Nancy. 'We feel as if we've known you forever. Ellie talks about you all the time.'

'Oh, does she?' Lucy flushed with pleasure.

'She says you're a brilliant gymnast,' said Tam, and Lucy's eyes widened until they were as big as saucers.

'The way I see it, we're practically family,' said Nancy. 'Which is good because I've always wanted a sister. Having a brother is so overrated.'

Tam punched her on the arm. 'I'm totally outnumbered by girls now, aren't I?'

'Yup,' said Nancy. 'Which means you have to do everything you're told. Isn't that right, Lucy?'

Lucy managed a shy giggle.

'I've been trying to look after Ellie for you,' Nancy went on. 'But I don't think I'm as good a roomie as you are. Apparently I snore! And talk in my sleep!'

'Ooh – me too!'

Just then Ellie caught sight of Mum, who hurried over to envelop her in a giant bear hug. 'Oh, darling! It's so good to see you,' she said, crushing Ellie tight against her. 'And I can't tell you how sorry I am for giving you my spots!'

'It wasn't your fault,' said Ellie, once Mum had released her. 'Mum – meet Tam – and Nancy.'

'Welcome to Cornwall!' Mum declared, giving them both hugs too. 'I'm afraid it's going to be a bit of a squish in Trengilly Cottage with all three of you girls sharing a room. And, Tam, you're on the sofa. I hope that's OK?'

'I don't care if I have to sleep on the beach,' said Tam. 'It's going to be so much fun!'

'Nancy wants to learn how to row,' said Ellie as they all clambered into the battered old Land Rover, somehow cramming all their bags – including Nancy's giant neon purple suitcase – into the back alongside paint pots, a pair of oars and a couple of lobster baskets.

'Ooh – I'll teach you!' said Lucy. As Lucy started

to tell Nancy all about the boats and the regatta that was coming up, Ellie leaned back and sighed, 'It's good to be home!'

The drive from the station to the house lasted about half an hour. The journey took them down winding country lanes, too narrow for two cars to pass. The hedgerows were already full of flowers. Every now and again a gap would reveal a view over the fields down towards the creek.

Finally they drove through a battered-looking wooden gate and drew up in front of a white-washed cottage with tiny windows high up in the eaves and an old slate roof, which looked as if it had withstood centuries of sea-storms. The windows were painted in a cheerful blue colour, and beyond the cottage itself the creek was laid out in front of them like a scene from a painting, shining in the spring sunshine.

'This is . . . it's too beautiful to be real!' said Nancy.

Ellie climbed out of the Land Rover and took in

her childhood home. She didn't think she'd ever been so happy to see the creek. 'It is like a little bit of heaven, isn't it?'

CHAPTER
Twenty-five

Mum insisted on settling Tam and Nancy in before she would let Lucy drag them down to the water. This mainly involved plying them with a strange-looking lemon-and-marshmallow cake she had baked in their honour. To Ellie's relief, it tasted better than it looked.

Then Dad emerged from his workshop and Ellie ran to wrap her arms round him.

'Good to have you back, kiddo!' he said, his eyes crinkled in a smile that Ellie had missed more than she could say.

After he'd been introduced to the twins, Dad

started telling Ellie about the new racing dinghy he'd been building. 'She's a beauty. Twenty-footer – I'd like your thoughts on the colour.'

'Dad! We haven't even taken Tam and Nancy to the beach yet,' said Lucy, who was jumping up and down with impatience. 'And the tide'll go out if we don't get a move on!'

'Better save the boat talk for another time, then,' said Dad. 'Time and tide, and all that.'

'And once Dad gets talking about boats there's no stopping him!' giggled Lucy.

Finally they managed to get away and ten minutes later the twins were having their first rowing lessons in the middle of the creek.

Lucy was with Nancy in *Roo* and Ellie and Tam were in *Jorian*. Nancy seemed to take to rowing like a duck to water, but Tam was looking pretty green as the boat bobbed on the ripples.

'Don't look so scared. *Jorian* won't let you down,' Ellie said. 'She's virtually unsinkable!'

'Didn't they say that about the *Titanic*?' muttered Tam.

Ellie laughed and patted the helm of her beloved boat. She handed the sleek handmade wooden oars to Tam. 'Ready?'

'Do I have to?' asked Tam.

'You can't come to Cornwall and not learn to row,' Ellie said. 'I learned when I was three. It's the best way to get around if you live on the creek. Actually, it's pretty much the only way to get around.'

Tam rolled his eyes. 'Seriously, aren't there any tube trains around here? Not even a night bus?'

Ellie giggled. 'Look, it has to be a symmetrical movement,' she explained. 'Make sure you angle the oars into the water so you're slicing not splashing . . . No, not like that . . . you're not slapping a wet fish!'

'You sound like my coach Robin,' moaned Tam. 'On a bad day!'

Tam had very strong arms from gymnastics, but rowing required a different kind of strength. The water resisted the pull of the oars with every stroke and if you didn't get the angle right it felt lopsided and twice as difficult.

'Stop flapping your arms, you idiot!' Nancy

yelled from the other side of the creek. 'You look like you're trying to take off.'

Nancy was sitting in the helm of *Roo*, rowing as if she'd been doing it all her life. Tam looked across and Ellie saw his face screw up in concentration, just like she'd seen him do in the park when they were practising and he was trying to master a complicated new move. He was obviously determined not to be outdone.

'Why not imagine the oars making the same motion as a rotation on the rings,' Ellie said, trying her best to help. 'It's the same swoop, catch and pull motion, only repeated over and over again. Yes, that's it. You're getting it!'

Tam had found the rhythm and *Jorian* started slicing smoothly through the water. He grinned in triumph. But then, just as quickly as he'd fallen into the rhythm, he fell out of it again and the oars started splashing in and out, making the boat rock violently.

'Uh-oh – I spoke too soon!' Ellie laughed. She leaned forward, put her hands over Tam's and tugged the oars back into an even rhythm before letting him try on his own again.

'So,' said Tam, his face creased with concentration. 'Did you get a chance to speak to Emma about your Grade Two? I meant to ask you before but –' he glanced over to the other boat – 'I didn't want to upset Nancy, you know.'

Ellie shook her head. 'She said we could talk when I get back, but there's nothing she can say really. I've missed my chance to get to British Champs and that's all there is to it.'

'Maybe there's some other way,' said Tam. 'For you and for Nancy.'

'Maybe,' said Ellie, but she didn't feel very hopeful.

'And are you going to ask your dad about your Aunt Lizzie and what really happened at the Olympics?' Tam went on as Ellie leaned over and tugged on the left oar to stop him colliding with a floating buoy. 'You know, find out what Scarlett's going on about.'

Ellie shrugged. 'I'm not sure I want to know. I

mean . . .' She hesitated, glancing over to the little beach and the boatshed where her dad was busy restoring an old fishing skiff. 'I hate the idea that she let everyone down.'

'But you don't know that she did. And wouldn't it be better to know either way?'

'I don't know. The thing is . . .' She struggled to explain. 'All this time I've been trying to follow in Lizzie's footsteps. But maybe I need to try to forget about her and do this my own way.'

'I suppose,' said Tam.

'And talking about going your own way – which way are *you* going? You're just about to get us stuck in the bushes!'

'How do I turn?' asked Tam, almost dropping one of the oars as he churned at the water, making them go faster in the wrong direction.

'Here.' Ellie was laughing. 'Just use one oar. Like this.'

Tam stabbed the water with the left oar, but *Jorian* just started going round and round in circles, still drifting towards a clump of bushes by the bank.

In the other boat, Nancy was doubled up with laughter. 'You're going to get stuck in the trees, you idiot!'

'No, we're not!' Tam yelled, although *Jorian* was getting closer and closer to the bank every second.

Tam shoved extra hard with his oar, lost his grip on it and it slid out of his hand and into the water.

'Oh, no!' Tam tried to lean over the edge of the boat to grab the oar, but it was floating just out of reach.

'Wait!' said Ellie. 'I'll get it.'

They were right up close to the bank now and Ellie grabbed hold of one of the overhanging branches to try to steady the boat. She reached again for the oar, but it had started drifting upstream in the opposite direction. She could feel the motion of the water pulling the boat out from under her feet, and the branch she was clinging on to creaked alarmingly. Tam grabbed hold of her legs, but that just seemed to make *Jorian* rock more and more.

'Let go!' he was saying. 'I've got you.'

'Don't worry. I can do it.' And for a second Ellie

thought she could, but just then a sudden gust of wind tugged the boat upstream. At the same moment the tree branch gave way with a crack and Ellie felt herself falling and dragging Tam in with her.

She'd taken plenty of tumbles in the gym, and she'd had her fair share of dunkings in the cold creek too, but the shock of the cold, salty water still made her gasp. Her head was underwater for a few seconds and then she resurfaced to see Tam spluttering next to her and, across the water, Nancy and Lucy rocking with laughter.

'Your first creek dunking!' Ellie giggled, unable to contain her laughter.

'It's freezing!' Tam's hair was plastered over his face and it had bits of seaweed stuck in it, but he was grinning. 'And I swear a crab just bit my toes!'

Ellie grabbed hold of *Jorian*'s side and tugged herself back inside then reached out a hand to Tam who landed flat on his face on the hull of the boat. They were both soggy and smeared with creek mud, but Ellie realised she hadn't laughed this hard in weeks.

Eventually, they managed to get the oar back, using the remaining one as a paddle to scoop it out. Once Ellie had both oars again and they were clear of the bushes, she turned to Tam and grinned. 'I'll take over, shall I?'

'Probably best!' Tam said, shaking himself like a wet puppy and showering Ellie with muddy water. 'How can it be so cold in there when the sun's shining?'

'Oh – it takes the whole summer for creek to warm up,' said Ellie. 'It's quite nice by about September. And you do realise you're supposed to try to stay out of the water – not throw yourself in the whole the time, right? That's kind of the point!'

'Hmm,' said Tam. 'Not sure I'm cut out to be a sailor. But Nancy looks like a natural. Maybe you've found her secret ingredient!'

Ellie glanced over at her friend and wondered if Tam might be right. She didn't think she'd ever seen Nancy looking so happy as she did with a pair of oars in her hand. She'd said Cornwall was what Nancy needed – and it looked as if she might just be right.

CHAPTER
Twenty-six

After the rowing lesson they sat together on the beach, drying off in the spring sunshine. Tam and Ellie were wrapped up in musty-smelling towels that she'd found in the boathouse. Lucy produced a bag of Cornish pasties and a flask of hot chocolate.

'Don't worry,' Lucy was saying to Tam. 'You'll probably be winning regatta races in a couple of weeks.'

'Um – what's a regatta?' asked Tam.

'Oh, it's like a big fête only with rowing races and stuff,' Lucy explained happily. 'And then in the evening there's a talent show on the quay. It's the

best thing that happens on the creek all year.'

'It's about the only thing that happens on the creek all year!' Ellie added.

'Ellie and I always enter the pair paddles,' Lucy said excitedly. 'And there are rowing races for every age group – from five to ninety-five. You two *have* to enter!'

'I'm totally in!' said Nancy. 'What about you, bro?'

'You saw how bad I was,' said Tam. 'I'd probably drown.'

'It's the taking part that counts, though, isn't it?' said Lucy. 'And you should all do the talent show too. It's like *The Creek's Got Talent.*'

'Except without quite so much talent . . .' Ellie added.

'Hey!' said Lucy. 'I'm doing a ballet dance with Maudie Bruton from Port Navas, and Tiny Warren is doing his performing-dog trick again. You three could do a gymnastics routine!'

'I thought we were supposed to be taking a break from gym,' said Nancy, the despondent expression crossing her face again. 'I get depressed when I think about doing even a forward roll.'

'But it could be fun!' said Ellie. 'The three of us, doing a routine together. And it's not like there are going to be any Academy coaches in the audience scoring our routine.'

'Where is the talent show anyway?' asked Tam.

Ellie glanced at her sister. 'Well, now that's the tricky bit,' said Ellie. 'It takes place on the Sailing Club quay.'

'Which means what exactly?'

'Well, it's a good-sized space for a gym routine,' said Lucy. 'It's pretty square – and it's grass not sand . . .'

'But?' said Tam. 'I'm sensing a "but" here.'

'But it's surrounded on three sides by water,' said Lucy, grinning.

'Which means if you go out of bounds on a tumble sequence . . .' said Ellie.

'We go head over heels into the creek!' Tam grimaced.

'Well, um – yes!' said Ellie.

'You know how I am under pressure,' groaned

Nancy. 'I'm bound to fall in.'

'Think of it as therapy,' said Tam. 'If the thought of a bath in the creek doesn't focus your mind, then nothing will. And I should know! Come on, sis, it'll be fun.'

'Oh, please!' begged Lucy. 'We have to beat the Ekes from the other side of the creek. They always win everything at regatta and it's our turn for a change.'

'Ekes from the creek,' giggled Nancy. 'You're a poet and you don't know it!'

'So, you'll do it?'

Everyone looked at Nancy, who hesitated for a moment then rolled her eyes and said, 'OK – if you all insist!'

CHAPTER
Twenty-seven

The next few days were so much fun Ellie hardly had time to think about the Academy or Grades at all. As well as planning the regatta gym routine, she took Tam and Nancy to all her favourite haunts. They had picnics on the beach, a night camping on the island in Frenchman's Creek, fishing trips out to sea with Dad, more rowing and sailing lessons, crabbing sessions, midnight swims – they even took Nancy and Tam to have a go at surfing.

And Ellie was loving practising gymnastics on the beach again. She got up every morning before the others and ran down to work on the boat beam and her watery bars, and to practise floor moves on the cold damp sand.

It was after one of these sessions that she finally managed to have a chat with her dad about Aunt Lizzie. She'd come down earlier than usual and she could hear Dad hard at work over in the boat shed. It was nice to hear him banging away while she trained, and after she'd finished she clambered over the rocks and pulled open the door.

She loved the smell of Dad's workshop: fresh wood, varnish and sea salt. In the middle of the sawdusty room stood the half-finished scull of a sailing boat, fashioned from strips of curved red wood that bent round the bow in a way that reminded Ellie of a gymnast doing a backbend. She stood for a moment, watching her dad varnishing the hull in long, loving strokes.

'Hey, Dad!'

He looked up. 'Hey! Come to see where the magic happens?'

'Yup!' Ellie had always loved the boatshed. As a kid, she'd been fascinated to see how her dad could bring old wrecks back to life, or create seaworthy vessels out of odd bits of wood and metal. She went over and perched on one of the oil drums while Dad kept on working.

'Dad,' she said. 'There was something I wanted to ask you. It's – well, it's about . . . Aunt Lizzie.'

'Right – go on,' Dad said, listening as he varnished.

'Well . . .' She hesitated again. 'You know at the Olympics. The team finals – where she hurt her leg . . .'

'Yes. What about it?'

'It's just . . .' Ellie hesitated once more. She knew how much her dad had adored his sister and she didn't want him to have to hear the mean things Scarlett had said about her. But she had to know so she blurted it out quickly. 'It's just – well, what exactly happened?'

'Let me see.' He glanced up for a second and squinted through the sawdusty shafts of light as if struggling to recall. 'Well, she was carrying an injury, wasn't she. That's why she landed so badly.'

'She was already injured?' said Ellie in surprise. 'Before she even got on the beam?'

'Yes – the fall off the beam just made it worse.'

'Oh,' Ellie's heart sank. Lizzie had known she wasn't fit, but she'd competed anyway, even though she must have realised that might cost her team the victory. Why hadn't she let someone else go instead of her?

'Didn't she – tell anyone she was hurt?'

'No – she was determined to do that beam.' Dad smiled, stopping his work. 'That's the thing about Lizzie. She can be very stubborn. No stopping her doing a thing when she sets her mind to it.'

He returned to the varnishing and Ellie sat there for a moment before asking quietly, 'Have you – have you heard from her lately?'

'Last I heard she was doing something to help orphaned elephants in Thailand. She sent a quick email from an internet café in the middle of the jungle . . . or was it Chiang Mai? Anyway, she was thrilled to hear about you going to the Academy. Said it almost made her miss gymnastics a tiny bit.'

Dad turned round and looked at Ellie. 'She's ever so proud of you, you know.'

Ellie flushed, suddenly not knowing what to say – or to feel. 'I'd better go,' she mumbled hurriedly. 'The others will be waiting . . . but thanks, you know, for telling me. I'm glad I know the truth now.'

But as Ellie made her way back up to Trengilly Cottage she felt empty and flat. She'd spent years wanting to make Lizzie proud of her, but somehow it all felt different now. Scarlett had been right – Lizzie had messed up. She wasn't the heroine Ellie had always imagined her to be, and now a bit of her own dream was spoilt too.

CHAPTER
Twenty-eight

'So, are you kids all ready for the regatta tomorrow?'
Mum asked at breakfast.

Ellie couldn't believe they'd been in Cornwall
over a week, and now the creek regatta was just
round the corner.

'We signed Tam and Nancy up for the rowing
races,' Lucy giggled.

Tam groaned. 'I'll probably cause some kind of
boat pile-up – and make everyone else in the race
capsize too.'

'You have a point,' said Nancy, nodding seriously.
'Better make sure they have a lifeboat ready.'

'No way, Tam,' said Lucy loyally. 'You're much better than when you first arrived.'

'I could hardly be much worse!' smiled Tam. 'And it doesn't help that Nancy is a natural.'

'Nancy's a better rower than I am!' said Ellie. 'And I've been doing it since I was tiny, so if anyone should be embarrassed it's me.'

Nancy flushed happily and said something about beginner's luck. But the truth was she had picked up everything to do with boats in no time at all. She just seemed to have an intuitive feel for it. Her strength and flexibility from gymnastics training really helped, but it was her confidence in a boat that was really remarkable. And she just seemed so happy on the water. She was more excited about the regatta than any of the rest of them, which was funny since recently every other competition had turned Nancy into a nervous wreck.

They were still talking about the regatta down at the beach later. Tam had lit a fire on the sand and they were toasting marshmallows over it. The evening was so warm they were still in their T-shirts, and the creek was like a dark, velvet carpet with twinkling lights reflected in it from the houses along the shore.

'Your routine for the talent show's going to be amazing, isn't it!' said Lucy, holding a marshmallow so close to the flames that it caught fire and she had to shake it hard to put it out.

'Or a complete wash out!' said Nancy. 'You saw what happened when we did a dress rehearsal today . . .'

Lucy giggled, remembering both Nancy and Ellie tumbling into the cold water when they'd missed their footing.

'But Tam's bit is brilliant!' said Ellie, thinking of the incredible new moves Tam had been working on. 'And we'll all totally stick our landings on Saturday night.'

'Forget about the talent show,' said Nancy. 'I want to win a rowing cup – and not the novice one either. I'm going to enter the main race with all the locals, and if I could win that I don't think I'd even care if they kicked me out of the Academy.'

'There's no way they're going to kick you out, sis!' said Tam.

Nancy shrugged. 'I'm not so sure. The Academy only gives you so many chances and then you're out.'

At Nancy's words, Ellie felt her heart drop to the pit of her stomach. Suddenly she didn't want the sticky marshmallow that she'd been toasting. Nancy was right – the regatta was just a distraction. In just a few days they were going back to the Academy and then she'd find out if her own chances were up.

But before she could start to worry too much about it, Tam jumped to his feet and said, 'There's only one way to get rid of these pre-regatta jitters! Who's for a moonlight swim?'

'Ooh! Me! Me!' squeaked Lucy.

'No thanks,' said Nancy. 'I spent quite enough time in that freezing water today!'

'Don't be a wimp,' said Tam. 'The water's not *that* cold when you get used to it.'

'Well, you've had more chance to get used to it than me,' Nancy retorted. 'Cos you capsize so often!'

203

'Oh, come on, Nancy!' said Lucy. 'Moonlight swims are the best.'

'And it is a perfect night for it,' said Ellie. 'Look.'

They all glanced up at the full moon and the star-filled sky.

'Fine!' said Nancy. 'But only so I can prove I'm a faster swimmer than Tam.'

'You're on,' said Tam, dashing down towards the waves. 'Come on, girls! Last one in the water is a loser!'

CHAPTER
Twenty-nine

Regatta day dawned bright and clear. The slight wind blowing up the estuary was perfect for rowing races.

Tam, who had been secretly hoping for thunder and lightening, barely managed to restrain a groan. 'You've got the lifeguard on speed dial, right?'

'Don't be silly,' said Lucy. 'No one's ever drowned at the creek regatta!'

'Well then, I'll probably be the first!' he replied with a wink.

The regatta was held at the sailing club on the other side of the creek, so after lunch Ellie, Lucy,

Nancy and Tam took the boats across the water. Mum and Dad drove the long way round, armed with plates of cakes and some of Mum's paintings, which she hoped to sell to tourists.

They moored the boats on the long pontoons in front of the sailing club and scrambled on to the old stone quay, which was decorated with bunting made out of old signal flags.

Dotted all over the quay and in the field behind the sailing club were little stalls – a tombola, a cake stand, Mum's art stall, face-painting and even a bouncy castle. There were children's running races in the field, and the smell of hog roast rose from the sailing club itself.

'But that's all just a sideshow,' Lucy explained. 'The really fun bit is the races themselves. And our pairs race is up first, Ellie!'

'Ok, so what's the game plan?' said Nancy, who was taking the whole thing very seriously. 'You'll need a strategy to beat these Ekes, or whatever they're called.'

'You do realise this is just meant to be fun?' Ellie laughed.

'No way! There is Trengilly and Moffat honour at stake here!' said Tam, doing his best impression of Emma before team try-outs. 'I want every single one of you to bring your A game!' he said fiercely.

'OK, I'll try my best, coach!' giggled Ellie.

She did try her best – and so did Lucy – but despite their efforts (and the very vocal support from Tam and Nancy) the Eke sisters slipped over the finish line in first place, as usual, and Ellie and Lucy came in fourth. But as they rejoined the twins on the quay, they were both smiling. 'Ellie reckons fourth is the new first,' grinned Lucy happily.

'And now all our hopes rest on you, Nancy and Tam,' said Ellie. 'Reckon you can do it for Team Trengilly/Moffat?'

'I suppose if there was a freak storm that sank every other boat in the race I *might* stand a chance,' said Tam. 'But even then . . .'

Just as he predicted, Tam's race was a total

disaster. He managed to bash into another boat before the starters' gun had even gone off, then got his oars muddled up so he rowed in the wrong direction for several metres before managing to turn the boat round. Then he got blown off course in the middle of the creek and had to be accompanied across the finish line by the rescue boat, to hoarse cheers from the others. The only thing he managed not to do was capsize!

'Which is a miracle because a week ago I'd have been swept out to open sea,' he laughed, clutching his wooden spoon – awarded for last place – with pride.

'And eaten by a shark,' added Nancy cheerfully. 'That's what I had my money on!'

The final race of the day was Nancy's.

'Come on then, sis,' said Tam. 'Time to show these locals what you've got.'

Ellie glanced at Nancy, half expecting her to have a last-minute attack of the nerves. But Nancy wore a calm, determined expression that Ellie had never seen before. 'She used to be like this at gym competitions,' said Tam as they watched Nancy clamber into *Roo*.

'Really?' said Ellie, surprised.

'Yeah – completely. When Nancy was little, she was cool as a cucumber at comps – and totally set on winning too.'

'What happened?'

'I don't really know,' said Tam as Nancy rowed out to the start line with clean measured strokes. 'I mean, look at her now. If she'd been half this focused at Grades, she'd have aced it.'

Ellie looked at Nancy. She was wearing a sparkly T-shirt with a pair of Tam's old shorts. But despite her comical appearance, she rowed with ease and assurance and there wasn't a trace of anxiety on her face – just a frown of concentration.

'Watch out for Fiona Trelisk from Helford,' Lucy was telling Nancy as she turned the boat close to shore. 'She'll try to bump you off course. Oh, and Joe Bruton from Port Navas is pretty fast, so you'll need to look out for him too. And that Eke boy, of course.'

'May the best man win!' shouted Tam.

'Or the best girl,' Nancy shouted back.

'See what I mean?' said Tam, grinning at Ellie.

The race got off to an exciting start with all the boats jostling to get into a good position. Nancy narrowly avoided an early collision and had to veer quickly to the right before managing to steer herself back on course.

Just before the halfway flag, Fiona Trelisk tried to bump her from behind, but Nancy turned her left oar quickly and managed to break free, sending Fiona spinning off and crashing into another boat behind her.

But Nancy had lost ground and Joe Bruton – who was small but quick in a little peanut boat – was coming up on port side, so she had to swing wide round the flag to carve a free course.

'Come on, Nancy!' screamed Ellie, Tam and Lucy in unison.

As the boats rounded the flag, Charlie Eke was in the lead, with Nancy and Joe Bruton hot on his tail. Now it was a clear water sprint between the three boats. Both boys were fast, but they looked as if they might be starting to tire, whereas Nancy – who had spent years of her life building up stamina in the gym – seemed to have endless reserves of strength. And, from the look on her face, it was clear she hadn't given up yet.

'She's catching the Eke boy!' squeaked Lucy.

Nancy's face was set in grim determination. She'd pulled clear of Joe Bruton's boat, but Charlie Eke still had half a length's lead on her, with the finish line now in sight.

'Go, Nancy, go!' yelled Tam. Ellie was screaming Nancy's name and Lucy was jumping up and down.

Nancy was drawing level . . . the two boats were now almost nose to nose. Charlie Eke was soaked in sweat and looked exhausted, but was clearly determined not to be beaten by a girl from out of town. But with just a few metres to go it looked like it was going to be a photo finish.

Ellie felt as if her lungs might explode in the last seconds of the race as Nancy put on a final spurt of energy. Somehow, incredibly, she edged ahead at the very last second, pulling *Roo* across the line just a fraction in the lead. Ellie, Tam and Lucy went wild, hugging each other and jumping for joy – so much so that they nearly toppled into the creek!

CHAPTER
Thirty

When it was all over, Ellie, Tam, Nancy and Lucy sat on the balcony of the sailing club munching hot dogs and running over every second of every race as they watched the sun go down over the creek.

'The post-race analysis is the best bit of the whole day,' Tam insisted as he recounted - for the fourth time - how he had been cheated of the gold medal by cruel fate and unlucky tides.

'Ahem - I think you'll find there's only one person wearing a medal today!' said Nancy, who hadn't stopped smiling since she'd crossed the finish line.

'Dad reckons it must be the first time in regatta history that a non-Cornishman has won a race,' said Lucy. 'Or non-Cornishgirl, in your case.'

'You'll have to come every year now to defend your title, you know!' said Ellie happily.

'Just try and stop me,' said Nancy.

Below them the stalls had been packed away and the stage was being set for the talent show.

'I can't wait to see your routine,' Lucy was saying. 'You'll blow everyone away with your gymnastic fantastic-ness, and Fran will be totally proud of you, Ellie!'

Ellie looked up in surprise. 'Fran's going to be there?'

'Oh, didn't I tell you?' said Lucy. 'She wasn't sure she'd make it because she has visitors or something, but when I told her you'd be performing she said she wouldn't miss it for the world.'

Ellie felt suddenly nervous at the thought of her old gym teacher watching. Fran had been away so Ellie hadn't been able to meet up with her since she'd been home and she couldn't shake the feeling that she'd let her old coach down by not making it to British Champs.

But there was no time to worry about it now. The quay had been strung with fairy lights that reflected on the water to create a myriad stars. And rows of spectators were starting to assemble, sitting on picnic blankets and camping chairs to enjoy the local talent.

'Is it me, or does that quay look way smaller in the dark?' said Nancy.

'And does the water look way, way colder?' added Tam.

'I measured it,' said Lucy. 'It's almost exactly the same dimensions as the gym floor.'

'Yes, but the gym floor is sprung!' pointed out Nancy. 'And it's not in the middle of the sea!'

The sun had disappeared now and the creek was a black sheet of water. One false move and they'd go tumbling into its velvety blackness. Ellie shivered, but she wasn't sure if it was with nerves or excitement.

And then they had to hurry and get ready because

215

the show was starting. They darted into the sailing club and changed in the toilets – tugging off their shorts and T-shirts and slipping into leotards and tracksuits before heading back out. Ellie's mum and dad had brought a couple of picnic blankets and laid them out on the grass so they got a great view of the stage. Other spectators were dotted around on camping chairs or clustered up on the balcony of the sailing club. It felt as if the entire population of both sides of the creek was there.

There were lots of other acts before them, but Ellie could hardly concentrate on watching because of the nerves that fluttered more and more insistently in her stomach. And then it was Lucy's turn. She turned to Ellie and squeezed her hand before skipping on to the grass stage to take her place.

Lucy was performing a ballet routine with a couple of other girls to 'The Dance of the Sugar Plum Fairy'. Ellie hadn't seen her dance for ages and she'd almost forgotten that Lucy was a talented ballerina as well as a gymnast. Lucy moved with a natural grace that was entrancing to watch. She seemed older somehow and there was something otherworldly about her as she danced across the dark square of the grass stage. It was different to watching her in the gym, although Ellie couldn't put her finger on why. And as pride rushed through Ellie, it seemed to wash away the nerves. At the end Lucy curtsied with a giant smile on her face as the whole family, plus the twins, clapped wildly.

And then it was Ellie, Nancy and Tam's turn. They pulled off their tracksuits to reveal leotards underneath. Tam and Nancy were in their Academy squad leotards – plus shorts in Tam's case – and Ellie wore her trusty Cornish competition leo. Nervous, but excited, she and Nancy took their places in opposite corners, with Tam on the far side. Nancy grinned – she didn't seem nervous at all tonight. It was as if the rowing victory had given her a new confidence. Tam gave them both the thumbs up and Ellie smiled back. It felt so good to be performing here, in this beautiful place, with her two best friends, and as the music started she felt the last of her own nerves disappear.

Ellie opened the routine with a tumble sequence, running from one corner of the quay into a handspring full twisting straight front, coming to a flawless halt just centimetres from the edge of the water. Next Nancy and Tam spun across the quay, missing each other by what looked like centimetres. And then Ellie was on the move again, flying into a round off flick then a double twist.

Tam had choreographed the routine for maximum wow factor, and the audience absolutely loved it, clapping each sequence more loudly than the last.

But Ellie forgot about the onlookers. As she spun and danced and leapt and tumbled across the dark square of grass, she felt like a night sprite, winged and dancing through the darkness, trailing showers of light behind her.

Her final sequence was a round off straight back half turn walk out followed by a round off flick straight back full twist. And to make it even more complicated, Nancy and Tam would be on the move at the same time, with the three crossing at the midway point. It would look amazing if it worked, and it would be a car-crash if it didn't. If any of them mistimed their landing they would go head over heels into the cold river – and they'd never actually managed to get it quite right in rehearsal!

Ellie glanced at her two friends, who both smiled back. She took a deep breath, lifted her arms, then leapt into the sequence. She spun through the air, once, twice, three times, dimly aware of her friends hurtling past her as she launched into the final full twist.

Suddenly she realised that she'd misjudged it just slightly. She felt herself tumbling towards the water. Her feet came down with her toes on the very edge of the quay and, as she looked down into the inky depths right in front of her, her body betrayed her into a momentary wobble. For a second the whole audience – the whole creek – seemed to hold its breath. And then she brought her body sharply under control, turned and finished the routine with a flourish. It reminded Lucy, who was on the front row, of the flick of a dolphin's tail as it leaps through the waves.

And then the audience went wild. Ellie, Nancy and Tam stood in the middle of the quay hugging each other, breathless and exhilarated - hardly able to believe that they'd actually done it. They were safe on dry land - and Ellie didn't think she'd ever enjoyed performing a routine so much in her whole life.

CHAPTER
Thirty-one

As the applause died down, the three gymnasts ran off the stage round to the back of the sailing club. Ellie was aware that she was shaking all over.

'You were - that was - the most beautiful thing I've ever seen,' Lucy breathed, her eyes wide with admiration as she appeared with their tracksuits.

'I thought you might be in trouble on that last landing, Ellie,' said Tam. 'I've no idea how you managed to hold it!'

'And you nearly took my head off with that straight back half turn!' giggled Nancy.

'Oh, Ellie, it was so wonderful!' sighed Lucy.

'There's nothing – *nothing* – I want more in the whole world than to be able to do that one day.'

And then another voice from behind them said, 'Well, if that's what catching chickenpox does to your gymnastics, I might order up a dose for the whole gym.'

Ellie turned to see who had spoken and nearly keeled over in shock. Emma was staring down at them from the steps of the sailing club!

'E-Emma?' Ellie stuttered, stunned to see the head of the Academy there, in the creek, that night of all nights. 'What . . . what are you doing here?'

'She came to see me,' said Fran. She had appeared behind Emma, her face creased with anxiety. 'It was a bit of a last-minute thing – I didn't know she was coming down till today.'

'And when I heard that my Academy students were risking life and limb in a talent show I thought I'd better come along and see what you were up to,' said Emma, glaring at them. 'You do realise you could have broken a limb out there tonight. It was incredibly risky.'

'Oh, we didn't mean . . . that is . . . I – we're sorry. We didn't think . . .' said Ellie.

'Clearly!' said Emma. 'Whose idea was this crazy stunt anyway?'

'It was mine,' said Ellie quickly.

'And mine!' Nancy cut in.

'I choreographed the routine,' Tam added. 'So if it's anyone's fault it's mine!'

Emma looked at them all and narrowed her eyes. 'You know, Ellie, I wasn't exactly thrilled when I heard from Fran that you'd been training on home-made equipment on the beach, risking injuries. But this . . .' Emma paused, glancing from Tam to Nancy, then back. 'This was insane. Just the sort of stupidly risky thing your aunt would have done.'

Ellie could feel tears pricking in her eyes. She'd blown it now. Surely Emma wouldn't want her back at the Academy after this.

'Luckily no one was hurt,' said Emma, then she paused again. 'And I have to admit it was pretty exciting to watch. Gutsy too.'

Ellie thought she saw the trace of a smile on the

coach's face. She gulped back her tears.

'And all the greatest gymnasts take risks,' Emma went on. 'I've probably taken a fair few in my time.'

'So, you're not – you're not mad at us?' asked Nancy.

'I most certainly am!' said Emma. 'And if I ever catch you doing anything like that again, I will order you a month's supply of Oleg's disgusting health tonic.'

'Yuk!' said Nancy.

'Exactly!' said Emma. 'But maybe tonight was a good lesson all round. Nancy – you just proved that you can overcome your nerves if you set your mind to it. Tam, you show the potential to be a very great choreographer. And as for you, Ellie.' Emma's grey eyes rested on Ellie's for a moment. 'I thought at team trials that you were a bit too safe and clinical. But you just showed me another side to you as a gymnast. And it was better – much better.'

'Oh.' Ellie didn't know what to say. She was full of such a mixture of emotions she could hardly get any words out. Luckily she didn't have to.

'You've won!' Lucy shrieked. She'd been the only one paying attention to what had been happening onstage.

'What?' said Nancy as everyone turned round and stared at Lucy.

'You've won the talent show! They're calling you on to the stage! I knew you'd win.'

'Looks like we have got talent, after all,' whispered Nancy, nudging Tam and Ellie, and avoiding Emma's gaze.

Tam grinned. 'Personally, I think the genius choreographer deserves all the credit!'

'Go on,' said Lucy, gesturing to where the announcer was calling for them to come and collect their trophy. 'You need to go and take a bow.'

Ellie turned anxiously to Emma, but she just smiled and said, 'Go on! Get your prize. You deserve it!' Then she added, 'Just promise me you won't do an encore, OK?'

Too stunned even to speak, and with Emma's words of praise still ringing in her ears, Ellie linked arms with Nancy and Tam and the three of them ran out on to the starry quay to collect the winners' cup.

CHAPTER
Thirty-two

The next day they all slept in late then enjoyed a long lazy breakfast, clustered round the table in the kitchen of Trengilly Cottage, basking in the glow of the previous day's triumphs. Later they collected the boats from the sailing club and helped with the regatta tidy-up effort. The previous day's sunshine had been replaced by April showers and they all got drenched, but it was good fun anyway.

The next few days went by in a bit of a blur. Nancy had caught a cold and Tam vowed he would never step into a boat again. And the weather made it difficult to get out on to the water anyway, as the rain fell in endless sheets. They went out for long muddy walks or stayed indoors playing endless games of Cheat, which Nancy won every time despite sneezing and sniffling her way through every game.

And the rain kept falling. Ellie's dad said it was the worst he'd seen for years. Just three days after the regatta the roads around the creek were so badly flooded that even the Land Rover couldn't get through them. There was no chance of getting to the gym to talk to Fran about what Emma had said during her stay, and despite the happy end to the regatta Ellie was starting to feel nervous about getting back to the Academy on Friday.

But nothing was going to stop her training. Remembering what Emma had said about safety, Ellie kept away from the boat beam and the creek bars, but she was determined to carry on with basic floor exercises, even though the sand was so sodden that she frequently found herself getting stuck. Nancy and Tam told her she must be totally mad, but Emma's words had given Ellie the encouragement she needed and she was more determined to succeed than ever.

After one particularly wet session, she caught sight of Nancy coming out of the boat shed.

'Loving the drowned-rat look,' Nancy said when she saw her.

'Well, you look like you've been paintballing!' laughed Ellie. 'You do realise you were meant to be painting the boat – not yourself, right?'

Nancy laughed. 'Your dad's been telling me all about gig rowing – did you know there are only three hundred and thirty-one Cornish gigs in the whole world?'

'Sorry – has he been boring you to death? Once he starts talking about boats he can go on for hours.'

'No – it was brilliant!' said Nancy, and she looked as if she really meant it. 'You know, I'm going to miss all this. But your dad says there's a rowing club up in Barnes and he knows someone there so he's going to ask them if I can take a boat out every now and again. He's gone up to the house to find me the details and everything.'

Ellie looked at her friend's shining eyes and thought that Cornwall had done her the world of good.

'Ellie, Ellie, come quick! There's a phone call for you!'

Lucy was sprinting down the beach, her red hair flying wild in the wind.

'For me?'

'From the Academy!' said Lucy, coming to a stop. 'It's Emma. She's in Guildford – for Team Champs.'

'But why's she calling me?'

'That's just it!' Lucy had no coat or shoes on and was already drenched. 'Mia Rudolph has food poisoning. She can't compete. They want you on the team!'

Ellie was so shocked she thought she might collapse. 'Are you sure you heard right?'

'Yes, yes!' insisted Lucy. 'They reckon it was Oleg's health tonic that made her sick.'

'Poor Mia!' Ellie heard herself saying. 'She must be so disappointed!'

'I'm just disappointed it wasn't Scarlett!' said

Nancy. 'But the point is she wants you, Ellie. It's your big chance.'

'But you've got to hurry up!' Lucy said. 'The competition starts in less than six hours and Dad says it's going to take nearly that long to get you to Guildford.'

'But how am I going to get there? The roads are flooded,' said Ellie, feeling her heart quicken.

'Tam's got a plan,' said Lucy, tugging at her hand and pulling her up towards the house. 'Come on!'

The three girls raced back to Trengilly Cottage where a heated debate was going on.

'I've spoken to Fran and she says the roads are clear further up the creek,' Mum was saying. 'She'll drive Ellie up to Guildford.'

'That's all very well,' said Dad, 'but how do we get her to Fran?'

'She could walk round the coast path,' said Lucy.

Dad shook his head. 'She'd have to go too far inland. It'll take her hours.'

'It's like I said – there's only one thing for it,' Tam said. 'We have to go by boat.'

231

'Have you seen the weather out there?' said Dad. 'It's raining cats and dogs. I can't risk taking a boat out in that just for a gymnastics competition.'

'But it's not just any competition,' Nancy was saying. 'This is National Team Championships! And you don't get a call up to represent your club and say "no thank you".'

'Surely they can find someone else?' said Dad.

'Of course they can – any other girl in the Academy would kill for the chance,' said Tam.

'But the point is that Emma chose Ellie,' Nancy added. 'Even though she's only been there for a term and even though she hasn't passed Grade Two. It's a huge opportunity. We can't let her miss it.'

Dad looked at the twins and then at Ellie and frowned. 'I just don't like the look of it out there.'

'Then Nancy and I will take her,' said Tam.

'Absolutely not!' said Dad, and Ellie wondered if he was remembering Tam's disastrous performance at regatta.

'Well, if you don't want a shipwreck on your hands, you'll have to take her!' said Tam.

Dad looked from Tam's determined face, to the pleading expressions on Nancy's and Lucy's. Then he looked at Ellie – who was still too shocked to take it all in properly. 'Please, Dad!' she begged. 'Can't we just try?'

Dad glanced out of the window, which had a view over the creek. 'I suppose the wind's dropped a bit. It might be possible – so long as it doesn't start blowing a gale as soon as we get out into the estuary.'

'If it gets too dangerous, then we can turn back,' said Ellie desperately. 'Just please say you'll give it a go!'

Dad caught Mum's eye. She hadn't said anything up to this point, but now she shrugged and Dad sighed. 'Fine,' he said. 'If this competition really means so much to Ellie, I'll see what I can do. But I'm making no promises – OK?'

CHAPTER
Thirty-three

Five minutes later, Dad and Ellie were pulling on life jackets down at the pontoon. The wind had slackened a little, but the rain was still torrential and it was hard to make themselves heard.

'I don't want to head out too far towards the open water,' Dad yelled. 'It's too dangerous. We'll aim for the Ferryboat Inn. Your mum will call Fran to pick you up from there.'

'Thanks,' said Ellie. Her teeth were chattering. The shock, combined with the cold and wet, was making her shake violently and she could hardly think properly.

'You're staying right here,' Dad said, nodding at Lucy. 'I'm not risking any more lives than strictly necessary.'

Lucy tried to protest, but Tam persuaded her that she had a vital role to play. 'You need to raise the alarm if anything happens to us storm-voyagers,' he told her. 'If you don't get a call from us within an hour, call the coastguard, OK?'

'And I'm not taking you or your sister either, young man,' said Dad, giving Tam a stern look.

'But . . .' Nancy began.

'No buts. Your mum would never forgive me if I let anything happen to you. I'd never forgive myself for that matter.'

Tam looked like he was about to try again, but Ellie's dad shook his head. 'I can be just as stubborn as you, so don't waste time arguing. Now, are you going to help me get this boat ready?'

Dad was grim-faced as he handed Ellie down into the boat. *Diablo* was a 30-foot deep-sea fishing vessel that had withstood many storms, but today she seemed like a tiny paper boat bobbing on the boiling surf. Ellie didn't usually get seasick so maybe it was the nerves that made her stomach heave the moment she stepped on to the rain-battered surface.

Dad told her to sit down at the back and grab hold of one of the ropes whilst he got the engine started. Ellie tried to focus her mind on the competition at the other end of the journey.

'Are you sure about this?' shouted Dad over the roar of the rain.

Ellie just managed a nod as the engine roared into life.

'Course she is!' said Nancy.

'Now, get going,' said Tam. 'She's got a competition to win!'

'Good luck!' Lucy shouted from the beach, and Tam was shouting something too, but Ellie couldn't work out what it was. The words were carried away on the wind as the boat lurched out into the creek.

If Ellie had thought the boat was unsteady on the mooring, it was nothing compared to what she was like on the open water. As *Diablo* scudded forward she seemed to hit the waves as if they were solid objects, crashing into each one with a sickening shudder. The roar of the wind was ten times louder out of the shelter of the creek, and the spray rose so high they were surrounded by a wall of white.

Luckily, Dad knew the creek so well he could navigate it blindfold. 'Are you OK?' he shouted back over the wind. 'You look like you're going to be sick.'

'I'm fine,' Ellie yelled, although she felt anything but.

'Stare at a fixed point,' Dad yelled. 'It'll stop you from throwing up.'

Ellie tried to do as he told her. It was like spotting in gymnastics – staring at fixed point when you're doing a rotation to keep yourself orientated. But it was hard to find anything fixed as they came out of the creek into the open water of the estuary. The winds were even more savage here, and they seemed to attack the little boat, playing with it like a mouse in a cat's paw. *Diablo* keeled this way and that, and threatened to overturn more than once. Ellie was terrified that Dad would say it was too dangerous, that they had to turn back, but he kept battling onwards.

Ellie's hands were red raw from clinging on to the rope, but out on the horizon, impossibly far away, she could just make out the white shape of the Ferryboat Inn nestled against the shoreline.

'Land ahoy!' Dad shouted. 'But you need to hold on tight. We're going to hit white water before we make it.'

He was right and Ellie just managed to grab hold of the rope again as the boat flung them up in the air.

Once they got through the white water, things calmed down a bit and at last they managed to moor the boat off the pontoon at the Ferryboat.

Even more miraculously, Fran was waiting for them on the beach with blankets and mugs of hot chocolate from the inn. Ellie was shaking with cold, but she could only think of one thing.

'Are we too late?' she asked through chattering teeth. 'Can we still make it?'

'I think so,' said Fran, glancing anxiously at her watch. 'You'll miss registration, but I'm hoping, under the circumstances, that the judges will still let you compete.'

'They better had,' said Dad, wrapping his arm round Ellie. 'After what we've been through to get you there they've got to let you do a somersault or two! Now, off you go.'

'Aren't you coming too?' asked Ellie.

Dad shook his head. 'I need to get *Diablo* back safely,' he said. 'But I think I'll warm myself up in the Ferryboat and wait till this weather passes.'

Ellie looked up at him. 'Thank you,' she said, but the words didn't sound nearly enough. 'It was worse than you expected, wasn't it?'

Dad nodded. 'To be honest, I'm not sure I'd have set out if I'd known how rough it was going to get out in the estuary.'

'I'm glad you did,' said Ellie quietly.

'Me too,' said Dad with a smile. 'I know how much this means to you.'

'I promise I'll do my very best,' said Ellie.

239

'I'll make you proud.'

'Hey! I'm always proud of you,' said Dad, his sea-blue eyes serious now. 'We all are. You go and wow those judges if you can – but remember your old dad loves you, no matter what happens!'

CHAPTER
Thirty-four

Shortly afterwards, Ellie found herself sitting in the front seat of Fran's battered old Beetle, wrapped up in a blanket. She stared out of the rain-splattered windows at the road ahead, unable to stop thinking about the journey on the waves. She could still feel the jolts in her body, hear the roaring wind in her head, see Dad's face as he'd shouted at her to hold on.

Although she'd dried out, she still felt freezing cold and her hands were raw. And she was frightened. Frightened more than ever of letting everyone down . . . her family and friends after all they'd done to get her there . . . the team . . . and, of course, Emma. What if she messed up like Aunt Lizzie had done?

As they crossed the River Tamar that marked the border of Cornwall and Devon, Ellie thought of Tam and the fierce look on his face as he'd told Dad that he and Nancy would take the boat. The thought made her smile, but it didn't ease the tight ball of tension in her stomach.

Fran turned to her and said, 'So, are you nervous?'

Ellie nodded.

'You know, Lizzie always used to get very frightened before competitions.'

'Did she?'

'Oh, she was a nervous wreck,' said Fran. 'You should have seen her at the Olympics. She could hardly speak.'

'You were at the Olympics?' Ellie looked up at her coach in surprise.

'Yes, I was the reserve,' said Fran. 'Didn't I ever tell you that?'

Questions crowded into Ellie's head. She

desperately wanted to see if Fran knew any more about what had happened the day her aunt's career had ended. Without thinking, she blurted out, 'What exactly happened to Lizzie that day? At the team final?'

Fran was silent for a moment, and Ellie wondered if she'd been wrong to ask. But it was too late to take the words back now. Fran stared ahead, her eyes intent on the road in front of her. Finally, she said, 'Well, you know Lizzie and Emma and I all trained together?'

Ellie nodded.

'We weren't just teammates – we were real friends. We'd have done anything for each other.'

Ellie thought of Nancy and Tam – prepared to risk their lives to help her win her dream.

'Lizzie was the best gymnast of us all. She won Commonwealth gold, European gold, World Championships – every medal going. The only one she didn't have was an Olympic medal . . .' Fran paused.

'So . . . what happened?'

'Going into the Olympics, Lizzie was at the very top of her game. The best she'd ever been. You know she was on track for individual gold?' Fran paused. 'Only it was the team event first and that's where she broke her leg in the vault.'

Ellie looked up. 'I thought she broke it on the beam?'

'That's what we all thought too,' Fran said, pausing again before she went on. 'The thing is we were in gold-medal position, but the Russians were just a fraction behind us. In the third rotation, Lizzie went for a handspring double front which carries a 7.1 difficulty tariff. It was an incredibly hard vault, but she managed to land it. What she didn't tell anyone was that she'd hurt her ankle on landing. Afterwards she admitted she was in excruciating pain, but she just strapped it up and went on.'

Ellie was horrified. 'Didn't anyone realise?'

'We could all see something was wrong, but she insisted it was nothing,' Fran went on, her face creased into a frown. 'The Russians had pulled ahead, you see, so we needed your aunt to get a great score to secure us the lead. There was no one else on the team who had a beam routine that could do it. She knew if she pulled out she'd cost the team the gold medal, and probably silver and bronze too, so she carried on. She performed the most flawless beam routine, with an acrobatic series like you've never seen. It was beautiful. Then she did a double tuck front to dismount.'

Fran hesitated and Ellie tried to imagine the unbelievable pain of landing on a leg that was already broken. It must have taken fearsome will and determination.

'As soon as she landed you could see something was badly wrong,' said Fran. 'She stumbled and her face was twisted in pain. But she raised her hand to the judges, then she took a step forward and collapsed.'

Looking up, Ellie realised there were tears in Fran's eyes. 'She lost points for the landing but we still won the silver. But that was the end of the individual competition for Lizzie,' Fran explained. 'Worst of all, she'd made the break much worse.

The bone was completely shattered. She could never compete again.'

Ellie realised that there were tears running down her own face now.

'I've never really forgiven myself for what happened to her,' Fran said. 'I was her friend. I should have realised and stopped her.' She was still staring at the road ahead. 'I retired soon afterwards and started coaching. It wasn't the same without Lizzie. And then you came along and that was hard for me . . .'

'Why?' Ellie looked up at her coach, confused.

'Because you remind me of Lizzie so much,' said Fran, turning to her with a sad smile. 'I think that's why I didn't want to push you too hard. Gymnastics broke Lizzie's heart and I didn't want that happening to you. But I realise I was wrong to hold you back. Because I know Lizzie is so proud of you – and she wouldn't want *anything* to stop you following your dream.'

The two sat in silence for a long moment, both caught up in their own thoughts and memories.

Finally Ellie said, 'Thanks for telling me.'

'I should have told you years ago,' said Fran.

'I don't think I was ready to know before,' said Ellie. 'But I needed to hear it now.'

As Ellie leaned back and stared at the rain falling outside, she knew that was the truth. She felt as if a wound she'd been carrying around for weeks had healed and she felt lighter, happier than she had for ages.

'Now, Lizzie used to say the best cure for nerves was sleep,' said Fran. 'So why don't you try to get some rest. You're going to need all your strength if you want to make an impression at Team Champs.'

CHAPTER
Thirty-five

Ellie didn't think she'd ever be able to sleep again, but as they made their way past Stonehenge she felt her eyelids getting heavy. She only woke as the car drew into the gym arena.

'What's the time?' she asked, sitting bolt upright.

'Well, you missed the first rotation,' said Fran. 'But Emma's trying to persuade the judges to let you compete anyway.'

Maybe it was because she'd used up all her nerves on the stormy voyage earlier, or because all her fears about Aunt Lizzie had been lifted off her shoulders, but Ellie felt oddly numb as she sprinted up the steps to the arena where the competition was taking place.

She ran to the changing room and pulled off her stiff clothes whilst Fran went to find Emma. As she changed, Ellie caught sight of herself in the mirror. Her hair was plastered to her scalp, and she could feel sea salt clinging tightly to her skin.

When she came out, she found Fran and Emma arguing with a woman holding a clipboard. Emma greeted her with a smile, but the clipboard woman looked stony-faced.

'The judges don't know if you're eligible to compete,' said Emma. 'But they're going to let you take part while they find out. Now Bree has started being sick too so we really need you. Are you up for it?'

Ellie looked at her coach nervously, aware that the Academy's hopes now rested on her. 'Do – do you think I can do it?'

Emma smiled. 'Perform like you did in that talent-show prank of yours and you'll do the Academy proud.'

Ellie smiled. 'Thank you – for picking me. I – I won't let you down. I promise.'

'Go on – get out there and warm up or you'll do yourself an injury.'

Ellie was greeted with a squeal of excitement from Sasha as she made her way into the arena. 'You made it, pumpkin!'

Sian gave her a giant hug, and Sophia and Isobel told her she'd saved the day.

'Liverpool are in the lead at the moment,' she said. 'Without Mia's vault and Bree's floor we're going to really struggle to catch up.'

'But just wait till those Liverpool girls see what Ellie can do on the bars,' said Sian kindly.

Scarlett looked less happy to see her. 'You stink of fish!' she declared. 'And your leo looks like it's been pickled in seasalt.'

But Ellie had more important things to worry about than Scarlett. With Bree out of the competition, she was going to have to perform on every piece of apparatus – even the beam. She couldn't afford a single slip-up. And there was no time even for a proper warm-up. Just five minutes later, Ellie found herself lined up with a group of other gymnasts, waiting for her moment to perform on the floor.

As Ellie glanced at the panel of judges, she spotted Barbara Steele, the Team GB coach, a small, elegant woman, with her hair tied back into a sweeping grey chignon.

'Keep it clean,' was Barbara's advice to the gymnasts. 'Try to relax and enjoy it!'

Barbara looked down the line of competitors and paused as she took in Ellie's appearance. Ellie felt a wave of determination wash over her – she was going to impress this woman, and all the other judges too. She was going to show them that Lizzie Trengilly's niece had inherited more than just pale hair and sea-coloured eyes from her aunt.

Sasha had devised a new routine, which Ellie had planned to perform at Grades. Set to a piece of music inspired by old Cornish sea shanties, it was designed to reflect the movement of the ocean. Normally when Ellie performed it she thought of calm seas, of sailing on the creek in the summer sunshine. But today it was different: her head was still full of the storm, the crashing waves, the treacherous rocks and the towering salt spray. And her body reflected that. On the evening of regatta she had moved with beauty and grace; today she moved with ferocity and power that was electric to watch. She tumbled quicker and higher than she had ever done before, leapt further and spun so fast she looked as if might never stop.

'This is the girl who was late?' whispered one of the judges. 'Where is she from?'

'That's Lizzie Trengilly's niece,' said Barbara Steele, her eyes fixed with fascination on Ellie's angry little figure. 'She was trained in a little gym in Cornwall, I'm told.'

'She moves like she's battling the elements.'

Barbara nodded and said nothing. There was something about Ellie – something about the intensity with which she performed – as if her very life depended on it – that reminded Barbara of the first time she had seen Lizzie Trengilly, when she was an unknown gymnast from a tiny Cornish gym.

Once the performance was over, Ellie raised her arm to the judging panel and ran over to Sasha.

'The organisers are refusing to post your scores till they've figured it out if you're eligible,' Sasha told her.

'And Scarlett just took two tumbles off the beam,' said Isobel.

'Which means we need you to perform a clean routine,' Sian added, 'or we'll never catch the Liverpool girls.'

Ellie glanced over to where Scarlett was in floods of tears, being comforted by Sasha. She couldn't believe that the Queen of the Beam herself had come off. Ellie could just imagine what Nancy would have said if she'd been there, but for some reason she just felt incredibly sorry for Scarlett.

She also started to feel the nerves creep up on her, knowing that if the judges decided she was eligible her beam score would now count towards the team total. She stepped up to the apparatus, acknowledged the judges, then stood waiting for the green light. She could still feel the rocking motion of the waves underfoot and it made her feel dizzy, disorientated. But she closed her eyes and tried to imagine she was on Trengilly beach, in the pouring rain, on the beam that Dad had made her. As she opened her eyes and launched into her routine, she felt steady again.

And with all her fears about Aunt Lizzie gone, she realised that she was no longer frightened of the beam. She managed to perform the tricky flick layout and free walkover without a tremor. And when at one point she felt herself wobbling, she thought of Dad valiantly keeping *Diablo* to a straight course through the churning white water and that helped her bring her body sharply under control. To her astonishment, she finished without a single mistake.

'That was fantastic!' said Sian, giving Ellie a high five.

'We can't be far behind Liverpool now,' Sophia said. 'We already have four strong scores on vault. If you could just perform your bar like you did at trials, we might be in with a chance.'

'But we don't even know if my scores are going to count,' said Ellie.

Next to the adjudicators' table she saw Emma still deep in discussion with the organisers. Ellie was called over.

'I'm afraid the rules clearly state that late entrants are not eligible to compete,' a stern-faced gentleman was saying.

'But do you have any idea what's she's been through to get here today?' said Emma. 'Tell them, Ellie.'

Ellie was aware of the panel staring at her. Barbara Steele had come to join them and was watching Ellie thoughtfully.

'I-I . . .' Ellie stammered. She wasn't sure she had the words to describe what had happened, but she knew she had to. So she told the story as best she could – of the storm and the epic journey across the creek, of the boiling seas and the cold and rain.

When she'd finished, she realised that Barbara

was smiling, and even the stern official's face had softened slightly.

'Now that's the kind of fight I like to see in a gymnast,' said Barbara. 'Where exactly is this place you come from? Sounds dangerous to me.'

'Oh no!' said Ellie quickly. 'Even when the creek is grey and stormy it's still so beautiful it makes you want to capture it in every move you make!'

Barbara's eyes twinkled and she turned away, bringing the adjudicators together for a hushed discussion.

Finally she turned back to Ellie and said, 'I'm afraid you are not eligible for individual medals today because you were late, and rules are rules.'

Ellie's heart sank.

'However, under the circumstances, we feel that certain concessions should be made.' She nodded at Emma and smiled. 'So your scores *will* be ratified for the team competition.'

Emma grinned but Ellie was still confused.

'It means we're still in with a chance,' said Emma.

'Now all you have to do is show the world what Ellie Trengilly can do on the bar!'

Ellie had to perform her bar routine alone because all the other competitors had finished their rotations. The familiar nerves kicked in again. Ellie glanced down at her red-raw hands and saw that Barbara Steele was staring at them too.

'This is going to hurt,' she said kindly. 'Even with your guards, it's going to be very painful. But after what you've been through to get here perhaps you won't mind that?'

Ellie twisted her mouth into a shy smile. 'No pain, no gain, right?'

'That's the spirit,' said Barbara.

In truth, Ellie hardly thought about her bleeding palms as she performed. She was conscious that her bar routine was fractionally messier than she would have liked and her pirouette was nowhere near as good as she'd done at trials, but she managed the difficult straddle catch which Toni Nimakov had commented on – as well as a double front half out dismount, which she'd only ever practised on the creek and never on dry land. When she came off, Sian and the other girls crowded round her and hugged her tight. Even Scarlett managed a stiff, 'Well done.'

And then there was the agonising wait for the scores. The girls stood with their arms round each other, staring up at the display screens. She could see that the team from Liverpool were doing the same. Her floor score flashed up. It was good – and on the bars she did way better than she expected.

Which meant it was all down to the beam – Ellie's least favourite piece of apparatus. She would need to score at least a 13.7 if the Academy was to beat Liverpool . . . and she'd never achieved anything like that in her life.

With a sinking sensation Ellie had a feeling the dream was over. She hadn't done enough.

But then the score was up, and Isobel and Sophia were jumping up and down, and Sian was hugging her, and Ellie's brain was struggling to process the numbers. 13.95. It couldn't be right – there must be some mistake. There was no way that could be her beam score. But Emma was telling her she'd got the fifth highest score in the competition and her own personal best on the beam. And – more important than anything else – it was enough. Overall, the team had scored a massive 156.050 to storm ahead of their rivals by a clear two points.

And then Ellie found she was crying and laughing all at once, as all the emotions of the day seemed to sweep over her in a tidal wave. Her hands hurt, her whole body ached and her head was throbbing – but her heart was leaping for joy.

CHAPTER
Thirty-six

'So basically we saved the day,' Nancy declared.

Ellie and the twins were sitting in Mario's café, munching doughnuts and watching the first pedalos of the season take to the boating lake.

'Exactly,' said Tam with a grin. 'If it wasn't for us, you'd never have made it on time and the Academy would have lost. We should really have got medals too. Or maybe some kind of plaque: *In honour of the Moffat twins who came to the Academy's need in time of peril.* Something like that.'

'The Academy is forever in our debt now,' said

Nancy. 'Which means I figure Emma can't kick me out just yet.'

'She's not going to kick you out anyway, silly,' said Tam. 'You heard what she said about there being another way to qualify for British Championships for gymnasts who fail their Grade Two.'

'Sounds like a long shot to me,' said Nancy. 'I mean, no one's qualified via the Challenge Cup for years.'

'Then you and I will just have to break the trend,' said Ellie, who felt as if anything was possible after Team Champs.

'But have you seen what score we'd need to get?' said Nancy. 'I don't think I can even count up to forty-six – let alone score that high!'

'The point is it's a second chance, isn't it?' said Ellie.

'I suppose so,' said Nancy, pulling a face. 'Who knows, maybe my growth spurt will be over by then too.'

'And don't forget we've found a cure for your

nerves now,' said Tam. 'We just need to surround the podium with freezing-cold water and you'll stick your landings every time!'

They all laughed. 'You know what my only regret is?' said Nancy.

'What's that?'

'I just wish I'd seen Scarlett fall off that beam.' She grinned and bit into a doughnut. 'I'd have given anything to have witnessed the Queen of the Beam's fall from grace.'

'I think she was the only person who wasn't a bit pleased the Academy won gold,' said Tam. 'Just because Ellie's scores counted and hers didn't.'

Ellie sighed. 'You're right. I think she hates me even more than ever now.'

'Take that as a compliment,' said Nancy, wiping sugar from round her mouth. 'She only hates people who she thinks are better than her. In fact, she's being quite polite to me now she's decided I'm a total no-hoper.'

'Forget about Scarlett and gymnastics and all that nonsense,' said Tam. 'I'm going to prove to you two that even *I* can't capsize on a pedalo.'

'*You* could capsize in the bath,' said Nancy. 'I bet you won't stay afloat for more than five minutes.'

'Oh yeah? Well, you'd better hope I don't accidentally tug you into the boating lake with me then, sis!'

'You wouldn't dare!'

Ellie sat and listened to her two best friends. The first summer sunshine shone down through the trees and she could hear the shrieks of laughter from the boating lake and the distant rumble of the city traffic beyond the park. She smiled to herself. Because she'd found her secret ingredient – or should that be ingredients? Cornwall would always be part of her . . . but so would London now. She had come to love the noise and the smells and the craziness of the city almost as much as she loved the creek. And, of course, if it wasn't for London she'd never have met Tam and Nancy.

Things had worked out better than she could ever have imagined. She'd helped the Academy win Team Champs, her scholarship was safe and now

Emma had found a way that meant she might make it to British Championships after all. She still had a long journey ahead – and there were plenty more obstacles to overcome if she wanted to make it to the Olympics one day – but she was on her way.

And that was enough for now.

Acknowledgements

A huge thank you to all the wonderful coaches and gymnasts who helped me with this book, particularly Neil Burton and Amanda Reddin at British Gymnastics; Liz Kincaid, Gill Ford and all the girls at The Academy of Gymnastics in Portishead; as well as Hannah Whelan, Ruby Harrold, and the GB Junior team: Ellie Downie, Amy Tinkler, Teal Grindle, Catherine Lyons and Rhyannon Jones, for letting me come along to training and answering all my endless questions.

My most special thank yous go to Sasha Tilley, Emma Baskerville, Fran Ince, Katie Cottrell and all Elsie's wonderful squad mates (and their families) at Baskerville's Gymnastics Club in Bath.
You are all an inspiration and this book is for you!

Tumble headlong into . . .

★ **RISING STAR** ★

The stunning sequel in the

Somersaults and Dreams

series.